Fusion: Together We Stand

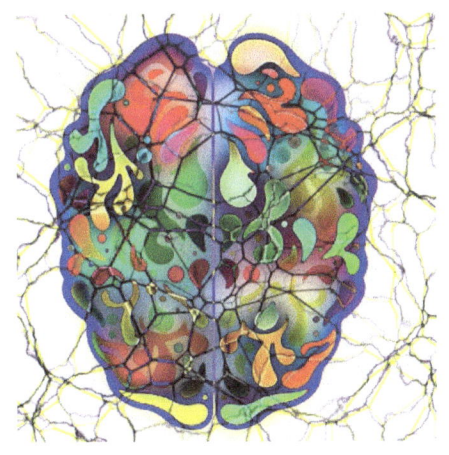

Curated by Sydnie Beaupré

TABLE OF CONTENTS

RED SETTING | MARTINE CRITCHLOW

BRANCHES | MARTINE CRITCHLOW

FOREST | SYDNIE BEAUPRÉ

TRUE NORTH | SYDNIE BEAUPRÉ

NO MERCY | SYDNIE BEAUPRÉ

SUCCUMB | SYDNIE BEAUPRÉ

MY LOVE | SYDNIE BEAUPRÉ

TEARS | SYDNIE BEAUPRÉ

PROMISE | SYDNIE BEAUPRÉ

ONE | SYDNIE BEAUPRÉ

SOMETIMES | SYDNIE BEAUPRÉ

BEAUTY | SYDNIE BEAUPRÉ

VICTORIOUS | SYDNIE BEAUPRÉ

SUCH UNSTABLE ENERY | SYDNIE BEAUPRÉ

UNTITLED | SYDNIE BEAUPRÉ

METRO DREAM | SYDNIE BEAUPRÉ

SHELL | MORGAN HILL

WORLD I SURRENDER YOU | NICKSON ODONGO MAGAK

ENDURING MOMENTS | NICKSON ODONGO MAGAK

TRIALS | NICKSON ODONGO MAGAK

DISTANT CONSTELLATION | NICKSON ODONGO MAGAK

LISTEN TO THE CANDLE | CHRIS FRIEND

DEVOUR THE SUN | CHRIS FRIEND

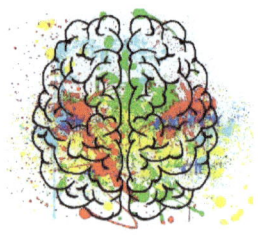

HIDDEN TREASURES
ARCHIT JOSHI

At 3:49am on a lonely night, Abinish Trivedi was wondering if his grandmother's stories on reincarnation had any truth to them. He desperately wanted them to be false. Seven lives? Here he was, considering his options on ending the one he'd been given. Talk about seven!

After having given a lot of thought to the matter, and having spent the past month riddled with insomnia and turmoil, he'd come to an absolute conclusion:

The brave thing would be to end it all.

Abinish had become a walking and talking corpse. However, he did more than just walk and talk. He took up valuable space. He spent his parent's hard-earned money on the engineering college where he wasn't performing well. He disappointed his girlfriend who was on the verge of dumping him, and he had long since forfeited his fading dream of becoming a poet. Simply put, he was a burden those around him wanted to drop, but didn't, out of politeness and affection. So the responsibility fell on him to rid the world of his pitiable subsistence.

The next day, he did his menial chores, and set out with his backpack. He stopped at an ATM and withdrew all his cash. College was not an option that day, as it was his last one among the living.

Money in pocket, he dragged himself to the nearest ice cream shop. The last one, he thought, then chuckled wryly. *People celebrate 'Firsts'... I'm going to be the one celebrating 'Lasts'.*

He bought chocolate chip, out of habit: his girlfriend's favourite. As he licked at it, he felt a terrible pang. How would she feel tomorrow? Would she recover? Did he have the right to bestow so much grief upon another?

No! He had to stay determined. Suicide is not easy, but he'd pull through.

He went to a dumpster to throw his ice cream away. There, he saw a skeleton passing off as a human being. It was a young, homeless girl, scouring the dumpster for some food. He gave her his ice cream. She grabbed it as though it was a pot of gold. She hugged him. In that moment, he felt the warmth of another human being. Another of the 'Lasts' he would celebrate.

"Your parents? Where are they?" he asked. She shrugged nonchalantly, as if not having knowledge of her parents was just another normal thing. Huh! The stuff people have to deal with! He had healthy parents who loved him. He could turn to them whenever he needed help. But this girl, she had nobody. She was all alone.

Life is cruel. It deserved to be short-lived.

Abinish ruffled the girl's messy hair, gave her a few bucks and shuffled along to a nearby bridge. He calculated the height of the bridge and the depth of water underneath. Jumping in would surely kill him. That was it; the modus operandi for his biggest mission.

He climbed down to the rough rocks that surrounded the water. Very good, they would surely kill him, those jagged edges.

His phone vibrated; it was Purvi. Abinish put the phone back into his pocket, let it ring. He was hardly in a mood to talk to his girlfriend.

As he started to climb back up, he found a devastated youngish man crying and wailing, lying sprawled on the rocks a few feet ahead.

"What's the matter, Mister? Can I help you?"

The man, in between bouts of intense sobbing, explained how he had recently lost his wife to liver failure. They were too poor to afford a transplant or find donors. In the end, he had to surrender the love of his life to poverty. Abinish helplessly consoled him for a while and set off to a new destination.

He would do one last charitable deed: donate his body.

At the hospital, he stared aghast at the scene. He had been to hospitals before, but this time something was different. This time, his eye caught the little details.

An impending death demands respect and awareness of life, he thought. If only more people realized they weren't going to live forever... Abinish gave a disheartened chuckle; he could write some wonderful poems about this.

Poems are for the living. He brushed aside his thoughts and concentrated on the task at hand. He looked around for someone who might help him with what he wanted. As he looked, he took in the scene unfurling before him.

There were so many people! He was shaken as he observed their faces. Some were optimistic, waiting for some miracle to happen. Other's had a blank, hopeless look, having lost someone. Some people had lost the use of their legs, some, their vision.

He saw a reception desk and hurried towards it, doing his best to appear older than he was. Asked for some paperwork to fill to register himself as a donor. The clerk told him that he'd first have to meet a doctor who'd check his health, blood streams, family history and some other standard policy stuff before allowing him to donate his body. Sizing him up, she also said he needed a parent's consent. Abinish froze. Was the game up? He awkwardly muttered an agreement and hurried off, snagging a pen from the counter first. His darting gaze looking for signs around the hospital, so he could find an actual doctor.

His phone vibrated again. It was his mother calling. This time, rather than just ignore the call, he disconnected it and thrust the phone back into his pocket. Parents and girlfriends. They were reminders of a life he intended to end.

As he set about to the doctor's ward, he began to have serious qualms again. He knew, even without the doctor's tests, he could tick off all the parameters the clerk had mentioned. Proper health, no disease in the family history, regular blood pressure levels, perfect eyesight... Everything was really alright with his world.

He saw a washroom and darted inside, needing a few private moments to deepen his resolve.

Abinish splashed water on his face and stared at a mirror. He forced himself to be firm on his decision. The mirror made it easy. Just seeing his repulsive reflection in the mirror reminded him of his sorry existence.

Just as he was about to exit, he heard a sob coming from one of the enclosed cubicles. Putting his ears to them, he finally found one the sound was coming from. He knocked on the door hesitantly.

The sobbing grew louder. He leaned against the door. To his surprise, it opened onto itself, revealing a boy sitting on the latrine. He was just a few years younger than

Abinish, and was shaking with grief. Abinish coaxed him out of the cubicle.

"What's wrong?" Abinish asked. It seemed a silly question; he was in a hospital after all. But this whole hiding out in the toilet seemed strange.

"My parents… my parents have been in an accident!" The other boy said, trying hard to compose himself.

"Oh," Abinish said slowly, not sure how to go on. "Are they…" He let his question hang in the air, unfinished.

"Serious. The doctors are doing the best they can. They even said that they will make it…"

"Hey, that's good news! It's all going to be okay, trust me," Abinish said, putting a hand on the boy's shoulder.

"I…I know." The boy wiped his tears with his sleeves. "It's just that I'm here with my grandparents. When the news reached us, they were really worried how I'd take it. Now, I can't cry in front of them, can I? It was hard for me to keep a straight face out there. I needed to… to vent. Came in here. Anyway, I must be g-going. Thank you!" The boy gave Abinish a sudden hug and dashed outside.

Abinish was numbed. Not an hour before, he'd thought he'd been cursed with the worst life possible. He wasn't even 25 yet, for God's sake! A huge chunk of his life was unlived, a mystery that would maddeningly unravel at its own pace. Had he seen enough of the world to take such brash decisions? His obstinacy had shown him a rare glimpse of a totally unknown part of the world, a world humbling and shocking at once. He fidgeted with the form he had been handed. He went and sat in the reception area, mentally exhausted, confused. The clerk eyed him suspiciously, but Abinish ignored her. This was not about the clerk; this was about him.

Should he do it? Even after all he'd seen, should he

still do it? *Could* he do it? After seeing the beggar girl warring with life all alone? Jeez! At her age, he had been whining about missing his cartoon episodes. Was he being as brave as he thought he was? Or was he being a coward? Meeting that man who had lost his love to liver damage, while all his own friends were destroying theirs with booze. A paper form reminding him he took for granted the things others were struggling with. Overdosing on sleeping pills or leaping of a bridge was the easiest thing to do. His body would take care of the rest of death. But carrying on, holding on… these were struggles of a valiant heart.

He looked down at the form. Several sheaves of papers stapled together. The last page was blank on one side. He felt that slight tug he felt so rarely when his poetic brain tickled him. Something wanted to come out, something needed to be expressed. He just put pen to paper on the blank side, and let the words flow:

"Oh Life! You capricious, conniving idiot! How childish your games of hide n seek! You hide away your beauty where most won't look. You hide away your values where most won't wander. You disguise your blessings as pain, why? But it takes an idiot to know an idiot. And today I realized what a big idiot I am! You're too precious to give away. Too enticing to lose. I will embrace you, and never let you go..."

He wrote some more. Then, Abinish called up his parents and told them he loved them.

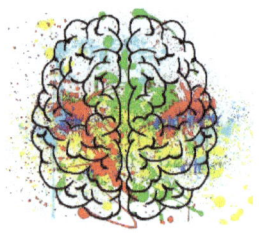

WIDE AWAKE

EMERIAN RICH

"Walter, wake up. Come on, it's time for lunch," the voice startled Walter awake from his much-needed morning nap.

Raising his head, he stared expressionless at the short blonde woman. The experts profiled Walter as a twenty-six-year-old, African American, non-verbal, autistic man with mild behaviors, but Walter felt like a man without a voice. Lazily following the woman into the main lunchroom of his adult daycare center, he sat in his normal spot and stared down at the unappetizing baloney sandwich placed in front of him. Why they insisted on cutting it into tiny bite-sized pieces everyday was beyond him.

"Walter's got baloney!" The hefty, red-haired girl next to him not only insisted on yelling when she spoke but did so with a half-chewed pickle in her mouth.

"He always has baloney, Sally," another girl at his table said, disgusted.

"No, he doesn't. Sometimes he has ham!"

"Does not!"

"Does too!"

"Quiet down girls," Walter's favorite teacher, Joanne

commanded.

No one could tell, but Walter was smiling inside. He liked Joanne's kind smile, shiny brunette hair, and the fact that she let him rest in the corner during exercise class.

Slowly munching on stale bread and room-temperature baloney, he bided his time until his next nap. This was his waking world: a never changing, ever-lasting, stagnant existence. He sipped on the generic soda his care providers had callously packed in his lunch as he surveyed the room. Pale yellow walls sprinkled with finger paints seemed to close in on him. Incessant mumbling from the greasy-haired beast seated on his left drove him to the brink of insanity. If only he could yell, "Shut the hell up, Phillip!" But all Walter could do was stare at the side of Phillip's blackhead-covered profile and wonder what the strange smell was that emanated from his dark blue, Chicago Bear's coat.

Attempting to ignore the miscreant, Walter turned his focus to the windows. Fake plants obscured his view outside. He wasn't sure if they were meant to hide the outdoors or hide him and his repulsive companions from the view of the general "normal" public.

"Cookie! Cookie!" A tall thin man ran by Walter, elbowing him in the temple.

"Stop Clarence!" A staff member followed the agitated fellow into the next room as Walter clutched his head and began to rock back and forth.

"Are you okay Walter?" Joanne asked as she approached him.

If only they'd go away and let him nap in peace.

"Are you done with lunch? Do you want to go to music class? Come on, let's go to music class."

Walter stayed put, continuing to hold his head. Music

class? More noise? No thank you!

"How about story time? Want to go to story time?"

Standing, Walter signed "yes" by making his hand into a fist and bending his wrist several times. Story time was a nice place to take an afternoon nap and the teacher never woke him. Walter followed Joanne into the classroom and took a seat at a large table smelling faintly of bleach and lemon. Laying his head down on his crossed arms, he closed his eyes. Peace. Finally.

Darkness engulfed him as sleep took over his body. Soon he noticed shapes moving in the blackness before him. There was a lighter blob to his right and a shade darker to his left. His being floated forward, reaching through the cobweb-like atmosphere. Wispy fog drifted around him.

"Walt?" a voice asked out of the shadows around him. "You comin' back?"

Walter focused his attention in front of him and saw the dim glow of a blue form he knew to be his partner, Mike.

"Yes, I'm here." The shapes around Walter started to make more sense. Feeling the pleasant sting of energy, he likened it to the brisk chill of a fall breeze on warm skin. He breathed in the electricity and delighted in the fact that he was back in his own world. In this world, he had no disability. His form emanated a blue glow, alerting others he was a friendly vibration.

His partner, Mike, stood before him. Mike's dark features became clearer as Walter's eyes adjusted to the dim light. Mike was a short blue energy force with a calm voice who always put Walter at ease. They never spoke of who or what they were in the waking world, but it was always understood that Mike was a constant in the astral world, whereas Walter would come and go. There was never much time to explore the subject more than that.

"Where are we?" Walter asked.

"The outlands. That last attack was brutal. I needed a place to rest until I was sure you'd be back." Mike's breath was labored and his aura was dimmer than usual.

"Sorry man, I wish I had more control over it." Walter gathered his energy and it vibrated off him. He placed a kind hand on Mike's shoulder hoping to give him a boost.

"Yeah, well, what ya gonna do?" Mike's breathing began to normalize.

Walter gazed out over the plains. There were many beings going in and out of these lands. There were those who didn't realize they were there and others who roamed without purpose. However, it was the ones that came with the intent to harm the innocent that he and his partner were there to protect. Those that meant to harm, though hard to catch, were easy to spot. Unfriendly vibrations glowed vibrant crimson, often so bright it was impossible to make out their features.

Walter had once roamed unaware and unconcerned with those around him. Some days he wished he was still oblivious to it all, but he had joined the fight because of his deceased friend, Stella, and he wouldn't give up if he could save even one person like her. Walter could still remember Stella's cold stare as her lifeless body had sat, dead, unbeknownst to the others in the waking world. He had tried to warn his teacher, but she thought he was just acting up and shoved his afternoon juice box and cookies into his grip. He had sat helpless across from Stella, absently munching on Oreos and watching the life drain from her face. Once the teacher had realized Stella was dead, there was screaming and pushing and sirens. Walter could still smell the fresh urine mingled with the dusty taste of Oreos. He couldn't bring himself to touch those kinds of cookies again.

Those same energy-hungry devils that had taken Stella, were after Joe. Walter didn't want to see another of his friends cease to be because of the greedy energy thieves. No, Joe was special. He had been a concert pianist, bound for the big time, but epilepsy had ruined his career. Joe came to the center with his portable keyboard and played Mozart and Brahms for a new kind of audience who didn't judge by looks or disability. Every day, when Walter was ushered into the center, he would seek out Joe and listen from a sideline chair to the wonderful music that poured from the electronic box on Joe's lap. Joe's kind of music was soothing. Not like the brash out of control noise from music therapy class. For a brief instant, listening to Joe, Walter would believe that perhaps one day, he would speak. One day, he might sing an aria or tell his care provider how much he hated baloney.

Until then, Walter would continue to fight for those like Joe who could not fight for themselves.

"Any sign of them near Joe?" Walter asked.

"No. We've been watching him for five months. I don't think they remember him." Mike stood, stepping closer to the edge of the cliff.

"They remember. They're waiting for the best time to attack, when no one is watching him."

"Listen, Walt, I watch him every day like I told you I would, but sometimes they don't attack the same person twice. No one knows why."

Walter ignored Mike's optimism as he continued to scan the horizon.

"There!" Walter pointed to a silvery-blue circle beginning to form on the valley floor in the East quadrant.

He streaked across the sky like a comet, hoping to guard the portal before Reds arrived.

"It's Gloria." Mike was right behind him.

Scanning the horizon for possible Red-lighters, Walter spotted one coming.

"Twelve o'clock." He sped toward the red-glowing being approaching Gloria's portal. "Leave her!" Walter roared in an authoritarian voice at the red-lighter, gathering his energy to the center of his form.

The red-lighter sped off in the other direction.

"Argh!" Mike exclaimed from behind.

Walter turned to see two Red-lighters zapping his partner's energy. "Clear off!" Walter slammed against one, knocking him into the other one. They rolled away and dissipated as Mike rose, ready to help.

"You all right?" Walter asked Mike.

"Yeah. They caught me off guard."

"Must have. Those were young ones. Wonder where all the big guys are?"

"I haven't seen any all day." Mike crouched on one knee, his aura fluctuating like a light bulb about to go out.

"Not even Bertha?" Walter neared his partner and spoke quieter as if the sound of his voice would injure Mike further.

"No. She usually comes to bug me at least once by now."

Walter contemplated why the Big Reds were silent.

"I'll see you tonight," Mike said.

"Huh?" Walter felt like he had lost some of the conversation.

"You're fading. See you later."

Glancing down at his lighted form, Walter sighed. He hated waking up.

\#

Unable to keep the mystery of the Big Red's out of his head that afternoon, Walter was especially non-responsive all through dinner. The care providers at his run-down group home contemplated his demeanor. Did he have seizures? They checked the chart, no, he didn't suffer from those. Did he get his medication? Yes. Did he have a temperature? No.

It was barely seven-thirty when he stood and went to his room. Climbing into bed, he heard one of the attendants say, "He must be coming down with something. Let him rest if he wants."

Eager to get back and help Mike solve the mystery of the Reds, Walter got into his favorite sleeping position and shut his eyes tight. Unfortunately, sleep would not come easily. He tossed and turned, wondering what the Big Reds were up to and who they were going to attack next.

He had several mini-nightmares of being attacked by the Red's. These visions made him startle awake, his heart racing. Dreaming, especially in nightmare form, was rare for him and he didn't like it.

When he finally phased into the other world, Walter woke to Mike's distressed voice.

"Walt, come quick, you gotta see this," Mike said.

Shaking the drowsiness from his being, Walter peered at the blue blur of his partner several yards away. Walter edged toward Mike, finding they were at the top of Consciousness Ridge. A large contingent of Red-Lighters was gathered below them.

"What's going on?" Walter asked.

Mike's energy level fluctuated, making his aura twitch teal, cobalt, and powder blue. "I don't know, but it's something big. Red's don't usually congregate like this.

What do you think they're planning?"

"Not sure, but whatever it is, we must stop it." Walter moved forward, preparing to dive over the cliff.

"Wait. There's too many of them, you'll be zapped. Mike placed his hand on Walter's shoulder.

"We can't simply stand here and continue to let them gather energy." Walter clutched his fists, his aura fluctuating wildly. Where was Mike's courage?

"Mike's right," a female's voice came from behind them.

Walter and Mike turned, seeing two blue beings like themselves standing a yard away. The two approaching souls were elder Blues.

"Greg, Sarah. We thought you'd be evaluating further out," Mike said.

"We were, but we saw the crimson glow and decided to investigate." Sarah's voice held an edge to it Walter had never heard from her before.

"What do you think is going on?" Mike asked, turning back toward the glowing valley below them.

"Haven't discovered yet," Greg answered.

"Strange, I thought I saw you up here alone a few minutes ago," Sarah said to Mike as she eyed Walter suspiciously.

"I was. Walter just got here. I've been watching them for about an hour, wondering what my next course of action should be." Mike still faced the canyon.

"Where were you, Walter?" Sarah asked, moving closer to him.

"I had a hard time getting here."

"You left your partner alone. You were much later than you have ever been. What were you doing?"

Walter didn't like the tone in Sarah's voice.

Mike turned toward the others. "I saw him fade in. He wasn't on this plane until just now."

"You haven't seen Bertha today, have you?" Sarah ignored Mike's comment and edged closer to Walter.

"No, she hasn't been around today," Mike answered.

"I was asking Walter."

"No, I haven't seen her." Walter wondered what he was being accused of.

"Why do you stay so close to Joe?" Sarah asked.

"I have reason to believe he's a target." Walter didn't like being questioned like a suspect.

"Did someone tell you he was a target?"

"What are you implying?" Walter asked.

Greg glanced toward Sarah and they stepped back.

"If you've got something to say, say it!" Walter's aura bounced between indigo and navy.

"Walt, come on man." Mike was right next to him and attempted to pull him back.

"We're watching you," Sarah warned as she and Greg faded into the black atmosphere.

"What the hell was that about?" Walter faced Mike.

"I heard a rumor today that someone saw a Blue-lighter flying with the Reds. Now, with all this happening..." Mike motioned to the Red's congregated below. "People are nervous. They probably just thought since you were missing...but listen, man. I saw you phase in and I know you're on the level. Don't worry about them."

Trying to bury his rage over being suspected a traitor, Walter focused on the enemy. Spying a way to collect more information without being seen, he pointed to a dark crevice in the side of the canyon near where the Red's gathered.

"There. Can we get there without being seen?" Walter

asked.

"Yes, excellent."

Both men closed their eyes and concentrated on arriving in the place without being seen. Soon, they found themselves in the small cave.

The hole in the mountain gave them the right angle to see and hear without being detected. Gradually the whispers and murmurs of the Red's voices began to drift into the cave. Walter strained to separate the sounds into some sort of understanding. Snippets of the many conversations going on came to him.

"All at once…together…attack… When the portal opens…he'll be vulnerable… When light first breaks… When half of them are awake… They won't be able to stop us all."

Walter could hear one voice above the murmur of all the other voices. It was louder and clearly deviant. He spied the Big Red hovering above the others.

Focusing on the voice, Walter could hear him say, "He will finally be ours for the taking. We've waited long enough, his energy is strong again." There was something familiar about the way the being spoke, but Walter could not place it.

"They're going to attack at dawn," Mike whispered.

"They're going to attack Joe," Walter said.

"Did you hear his name?"

"No."

"Then how do you know?"

"I just do." Walter continued to watch the Big Red he had singled out. "Do you know who that big one is above?" He pointed to the hovering elder.

Suddenly red light exploded into the cave from behind them, making the two Blue-lighters jump.

"What are you doing in here?" a red-lighter demanded.

"Uh… w-we w-were…" Mike spoke in a stutter.

"You friend's of Simon?" a second red-lighter asked.

"Uh, w-well um…" Mike's aura bounced with nervousness.

"Yes," Walter said. "But he told us to be careful. We can't be seen by the other Blue-lighter's watching from the ridge. Come further in, we can't risk being detected." Walter lured the two as far back as he could. "He gave us a message for you." Walter summoned as much energy as he could into his right hand and reached out into the middle of the red-lighter's being. "Die!" He used his energy to suck all of the Red-lighter's power into him. The red-lighter squirmed in pain, a howl issuing from him that would be sure to call the attention of the others.

Luckily Mike had anticipated Walter's attack and attacked the second red-lighter in a less violent, but nevertheless effective manner. As the two red beings dissipated, a surge of energy at the mouth of the cave glowed crimson.

"Focus on our domain now," Walter said. He closed his eyes and thought of his home base and arrived there a moment later.

"That was too close." Mike arrived next Walter in their normal watch area. Mike panted as he bent over, obviously drained from the confrontation. "I've never seen you attack like that. It was almost like…"

"Almost like what?" Walter faced Mike in anger. Was his own partner going to start suspecting him?

"Nothing. It just wasn't like you."

"We're at war, Mike. Sometimes in war you have to do things you don't want to do."

"How do you know? You've never been in a war

before."

"I saw it on T.V. Anyway, it doesn't matter. We got out and we're safe. And now we know what they're up to."

"We do?" Mike asked, taking a seat on a rock formation.

"They're going to attack Joe."

"You don't know that."

"Yes, I do know that."

"What do you know?" Sarah appeared a few feet away.

"They are going to attack Joe at dawn," Walter answered, in a proud and unfriendly manner.

"Is that what you think, Mike?" Greg was suddenly right next to Mike.

Mike swallowed hard, studying Walter before answering.

"Yes."

"Well, that's not long. I guess we should alert the others." Sarah turned to go.

"Yeah, you do that. And by the way, your traitor's name is Simon." Walter's tone was smug.

"Simon?" Greg asked.

"Yes, that's what they said." Mike's aura calmed as he spoke with conviction.

"We'll take care of it," Sarah said.

"See that you do." Walter turned from Sarah and headed for Joe's portal.

#

Blue-lighters could be seen, scattered here and there in the proximity of Joe's portal location. Although Walter and Mike rarely saw another pair of Blues in their sector, it appeared they had all been called there to help protect Joe and fight off the large amount of negative beings that were sure to descend on the area.

"I sure hope you're right," Mike murmured low enough to escape the other's notice.

"I am." Walter scanned the horizon for crimson energy.

However, as dawn came and went, uneasy voices questioned the intel Walter had provided. Sarah and Greg, who stood not four yards away studied Walter as if he were an escape convict.

"They'll come," Walter whispered, trying to ease Mike's mind.

"I don't think so, bud." Mike's aura dimmed as he spoke.

Walter couldn't stand the fact that Mike was disgraced by his conclusions, but he knew they would come. They had to come. He scanned the outer limits of the planes, looking for any sign of the Red's. A few quiet cracks of energy like mini lightning bolts struck here and there signaling the opening of a portal, but there was not a Red streak in sight.

As voices of dissension rippled through the Blue ranks, a burst of red light in the horizon silenced them all. Shortly after, a massive explosion occurred, rippling energy through the entire world.

"Damn it! They got Samantha!" Sarah shouted. "Go, go, go!" The other teams took off at her order, blue streaks filling the sky toward the event like reverse shooting stars. "You two stay put." She stared at Walter and Mike, repulsion on her face.

"How could you, Walter?" Greg shook his head in disgust.

"I didn't... I haven't..." Walter was thoroughly baffled by the change in course. Studying Mike's disappointed expression, Walter questioned himself. He had heard them plot to kill Joe, hadn't he?

"How long have you been working with them?" Sarah asked as she stepped closer to Walter. Backing up his partner, Greg stood on the other side of Walter, blocking him in.

Walter opened his mouth to speak, but Mike cut in before he could say a word.

"Walt might be a little obsessed with protecting his friend Joe, but he isn't a traitor."

A streak of cobalt crossed the sky and landed next to Sarah, forming into the body of a Blue.

"Samantha's dead," the newcomer said. The shock of a death on their watch made a hush fall over those congregated.

"I'm sorry, Walter, but I'm going to have to ask you resign your post." Sarah spoke quietly, but there was no doubt any of them had misheard her.

Walter nodded, attempting to understand what had taken place. He felt responsible for the death of the young girl, Samantha, but couldn't shake the feeling that the Reds were still after Joe. He retraced his steps in his mind, wondering where he had gone wrong.

"Mike, you'll be assigned a new partner this afternoon. Until then, sweep the area and inform me of any attacks," Sarah said.

Mike nodded as the others began to leave.

"And Walter, I strongly advise you. Don't interfere with us." Sarah's blue glow vibrated, energy sparking off her. Walter acknowledged the threat, backing away.

Once the others were out of sight, Mike placed a consoling hand on Walter's shoulder.

"Sorry bud."

"I heard them say 'he' not 'she'," Walter muttered. His aura faded as his sadness dampened his energy.

"I know." Mike patted Walter on the back as he made to leave. "See you around."

As his former partner and friend blurred into the atmosphere, Walter was consumed by the guilt of allowing an innocent to be harmed. He had failed his objective because of an obsession. He no longer felt like he had a purpose. Depression set in, causing him to return to the waking world.

#

Sitting quietly, listening to Joe pick out a classical tune on his portable keyboard the next morning, Walter dwelled on his failure. His feelings in the waking world had cost him the life of someone who truly needed his help. Disgusted with himself, he turned away from Joe and looked outside where Sally and Clarence were fighting over a yellow bouncy ball. Oh, to be so singularly occupied.

Manic giggling erupted next to him as Phillip smacked his legs in delight over a joke only he understood. His black-head covered face wiggled and churned as he chattered in his gibberish language.

Walter stood, taking a seat across the room. The last thing he wanted was to be seated by the wacky, muttering fool. For some reason, Phillip was always next to Walter, irritating him to the brink of insanity. Phillip's incessant laughter at all the wrong times was asinine. It always seemed like Phillip would make more noise when Walter needed to concentrate. Like when Joe had his last seizure, or when Stella died. Walter glared at Phillip as if his stare would burn him like an insect under a magnifying glass.

Suddenly Joe's music stopped and his portable keyboard crashed to the ground, playing accidental keys as it fell. Walter's attention snapped to that side of the room, studying Joe as he fell out of his chair. Staff ran to his aid, moving unsafe objects away from his shaking body.

Walter's heart jumped. The Reds were attacking Joe! Walter's feelings on the subject were instantly justified. It was Joe they wanted all along, Samantha was only a decoy. How would he get back to help Joe now? He couldn't fall asleep with all the commotion going on.

A loud cackling from the other side of the room broke Walter's concentration on Joe. Phillip was laughing uncontrollably and as Walter studied him, he noticed his eyes were rolled back to expose only the whites. As Phillip shook and laughed, tiny zaps of crimson electricity sparked from his eyes. Something about the chattering reminded Walter of the Big Red he had spied from the cave.

Phillip was a Red! Walter wanted to scream it at the top of his lungs. Walter opened his mouth, willing a scream to come out, but none did. He stood and facing the window, smacked the glass with his open palm.

Help, help! he wanted to scream, but he couldn't urge his non-verbal mouth to speak. Outside, Sally and Clarence paused their argument about the ball long enough to wave to Walter.

"Hi Walter!" Sally's irksome voice rang out.

Sighing, Walter rolled his eyes as he realized his communication skills in the waking world would never help him save Joe.

Behind Walter, a staff member said, "His seizure's going into four minutes, call 911."

Walter swung around, studying Joe's uncontrollable twitching.

I won't let you die Joe, Walter said in his head. There was only one way he knew to get to his world without falling asleep naturally. Turning toward the window,

Walter gripped the window sill with both hands and smashed his head into the glass as hard as he could. With adrenaline and anger on his side, he managed to crack his head on the glass pretty good. The blackness came quickly.

#

Once on the other side, Walter could see the mass of Red-lighter's congregated upon Joe's portal. Several kept watch while three of the Big Reds took turns diving into the portal and sucking as much energy as they could from the poor soul. When one got full, it would soar out of the hole, sparking and blazing with increased red energy. As if on cue, the next would plunge into the vortex and the process would start again.

Walter summoned all his love for Joe, his hatred for the Reds, and his fear of losing another innocent soul to evil ministrations. His energy grew until he appeared on fire. Blue flames erupted throughout his body and a crackle of electricity rocked the valley. The Red-lighter's guarding the portal stared up Walter unmoving.

"Who is that?" one asked.

"*What* is that?" asked another.

Jumping forward, Walter leaped into the air and zoomed toward the crimson glow. His being slammed into the congregation, but he did not feel his power lessen. Beings scattered away from the hole like pins hit by a bowling ball. He hammered away at them, pulling from their energy and becoming stronger as he fought. The Reds faded one by one. A few ran into the darkness around them, obviously afraid of what Walter would do to them. Walter noticed blue entities gathering at a safe distance. He prayed they would be smart enough to stay out of the fight.

Finally, only one Red stood at the portal and shook as

the energy coming from below coursed through him. His body was bright red and magenta electrical zaps erupted every few seconds from the top of his head.

Taking a running leap into the being, Walter knocked him away from the power source and landed with him a couple yards away. Walter held the monster down, growling with the force it took to do so.

"You killed Stella you bastard! I won't let you take Joe, too."

The Big Red grunted in anger as he was unable to move with the strength of Walter holding him down.

"I've already drained him," the chattery voice said. "He won't live past tonight."

"I think he will. You see Phillip, he's got friends on this side that will ensure he thrives despite your selfish attack." Walter pushed Phillips's head to the side and held it there so he could see the other Blue-lighter's infusing the open portal with their positive energy.

"I'll get him again. You can't protect him all the time."

"That's where you're wrong." Walter applied pressure to Phillip's head with his right hand and reached into the center of his being with his left. Sucking the energy into his own being, Walter willed Phillip's body to be drained. He didn't want the monster to be able to do any more harm.

Groaning, Phillip attempted to free himself. He fought with all his might to make Walter lose his balance or grip, but it was no use. Walter was strong and held firm, adamant that Phillip would not break free. Philip's aura flickered, fading until his form evaporated into the dark.

A victorious thrill filled Walter as he collected the energy swirling about him. He sucked in the crimson light as if breathing deeply after a rainstorm. A sigh of relief left

Walter and he stretched, feeling the strength he had acquired from the kill. His aura was purple, and he thought he must be visible from the waking world, he shined so bright. He had a wonderful feeling of accomplishment as he stood and enjoyed the new invincibility he possessed.

"Joe will live," Mike said, calling Walter back to the moment.

"Good." Walter studied his old partner who seemed small and weak.

"Glad you're back. I hope your old partner is willing to take you back." Sarah approached, Greg not far behind her. "On a probationary period of course."

"I'm not back." Walter stood tall; his arms crossed in determination. "I'll be working for myself from now on, protecting the innocent who seem to be overlooked by you." He turned his back on them and walked toward Conscientiousness Ridge.

"There's no need to—" Sarah began.

Walter turned back, staring squarely at Sarah. "Oh, and Sarah, I advise you don't interfere with me, or you'll have more trouble than you know what to do with."

Sarah took a step back, her aura fading slightly at the threat.

"See you, Mike." Walter grinned as he turned to his friend.

"Yeah, stay safe," Mike said, a weak smile touching his lips.

\#

As Walter lay in the hospital bed in a coma, men in white coats examined him. He suffered severe head injuries due to self-inflicted damage to his skull. The experts would profile Walter as a twenty-six-year-old, African American, autistic man who suffered a psychotic break, probably caused by the trauma of watching the near-death seizure of a friend, but Walter felt like a man who finally had a voice.

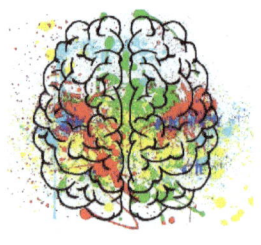

MY AMBIGUOUS LOSS

EMERIAN RICH

When you have a baby, your whole world changes. Everyone tells you this will happen when you're pregnant and it's one of life's solid truths along with death and taxes. Still, no matter how you prepare for it, or think you're ready, it always seems to catch you off guard.

My son was born happy and healthy, if a bit early, sixteen years ago. Despite complications during and after pregnancy, we were pretty happy for about a year. We reveled in the new baby smell. We giggled at his baby bandito burrito shape. We even smiled when he pooed. Every parent on the planet can recount these cute stories, whether you want them to or not.

At about a year old we realized we needed to get our son checked out. Even though he was a happy, energy-filled cutie, with the exception of speaking a few words at six months, he had completely stopped talking and hadn't said a word since.

We read all the books. At age one he should have been gabbing up a storm. Perhaps not Nobel Prize award winning sentences, but something. A mama or a dada or a baba—anything would've been a gift to us.

We started looking for a cause. He was super active, so perhaps walking provided a bigger motivation than talking? My husband had some jaw structure problems in his youth, perhaps this was the issue. I don't know my biological father. Could there be something on my side of the family causing this deficiency? Was he deaf? Was he mute? Did we feed him the wrong sort of formula? Was it the shots administered in the hospital? Questions plagued us.

We enrolled our son in a speech delay program and got him checked out by specialists. This time in our lives was devastating. Although birth defects and mutations happen naturally in more homes than anyone realizes, somehow, we felt to blame. Maybe it was because I didn't breastfeed. Maybe it's because we didn't spend enough time teaching him. Was it our fault in some way?

The real guilt set in. It's bad enough when you can't achieve something in your own life and feel a failure but when you've imposed a failure of yours onto another living being, it's soul crushing. You want to push the reset button and hope a do-over will come out better. Like somehow you could turn back time, change something you did—or didn't do—so your child could have a normal life.

The next few months were spent learning sign language and driving our son to therapy sessions. It seemed to be getting better, like there was hope, but then we were given the diagnosis. Autism.

It might seem overly dramatic for someone who hasn't gone through this, but our entire world shut down. It was as if our son was taken away from us. Every hope and dream we had about him growing up, going to college, living his own life, having a wife, and having his own children was taken away. I've worked with autistic adults and I've seen what some of them often have to go through. They live in care homes with little to call their own, bused out to work centers where they work for lower than minimum wage, with little choices, and little love. I know not every autistic person lives this way but my mind ran with the worst case scenario. My biggest sorrow when being told my child was autistic was not the thought that I might have to spend the rest of my life caring for him, but about everything he was going to miss out on.

My mother was supportive the whole time, telling me, "He's our baby and we will still love him, despite his disability."

Although the statement was true, I couldn't get over the grief of losing him as a "normal" child. During months of depression, I couldn't even talk about my son without bursting into tears. I held my head up high in public, while inside I was a complete basket case. I became angry and distant from others who tried to help by assuring me that they knew people who had autism and went on to live happy lives. Every time I shared my thoughts I felt dirty or like a bad parent. I was not saying I wanted to harm him, but there were times when I said, "Had I known he would come out with autism, I would've chosen not to have him."

The worst part was, I had no one to tell me it was okay to feel this way, no one to allow me to voice my feelings without judgment. No one understood. Even very close friends I confided in left me feeling like a murderess mother. They asked me if I was going through postpartum depression or if I needed to give the child up to someone who could take care of him properly. Believe me when I say that in the darkest moments, I did wonder if I should adopt him out to someone who was better equipped.

I remember one distinct conversation with my mother in

which she said, "Yes, I know, you feel like someone has died."

I replied, "Yes, but the body is still in the house."

Therein lays my ambiguous loss. If only I had known at the time that I was legitimately grieving.

Dr. Pauline Boss, Ph.D., defines ambiguous loss as one where there is no verification of death or that the person you love will return to the way they used to be. This is often a diagnosis given to family members who have lost a loved one in war where no body is found or like the families of the 9-11 bombings where no body was recovered. Your brain just doesn't believe it's real. In those cases of war and terrorism, everyone rallies around you. They say it's okay to cry, to let it out and mourn, but for the parents of a special needs child, you're told to buck up and deal with it. This is the hand you've been dealt and that's just the way it is.

I was shocked to find out I had been experiencing ambiguous loss for years. Sure, my son was alive, but the baby I thought I had, the dreams I had for him were no longer possible, or so I thought.

My hope in writing this is that new parents experiencing ambiguous loss are made aware of this condition and allow themselves to go through the grieving process without guilt. If I had known others experienced this kind of trauma and I was allowed to feel the way I did, I believe the healing process would've started sooner.

After my husband and I came to grips with the situation, we were ready to live out our lives with our special son. But until we grieved that loss, we could not move on to be the parents we are today.

Nowadays, our son is in high school. He learned to speak and feed himself and potty-train. He's been in speech, occupational therapy, and behavior therapy and with help, he has actually become a well-adjusted young adult who is pretty independent. I can even imagine him living out a life of his own now. We know he will continue to change with time. He'll have good days and bad. He may run for president yet! No matter what he becomes, he is our son and we love him just as much as we would any "normal" child.

For those of you out there who are going through ambiguous loss and feel like you will never make it through, please know you're not alone. Stay strong, keep moving forward, and allow yourself to grieve. It doesn't mean you are a bad person. It just means you're human.

If you feel yourself unable to cope, please seek the help of a professional therapist. Sometimes having someone listen and understand gives you the strength to handle the next hurdle.

For more information on ambiguous loss, visit Dr. Pauline Boss, Ph.D. at: ambiguousloss.com.

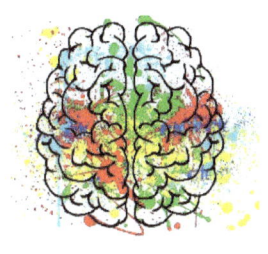

AUTISM

MARK HEATHCOTE

Autistic spectrum tries

Understanding the individual,

Their level of capabilities

It is a cognitional,

Symptom with social disabilities

Multifaceted: every one of them, original.

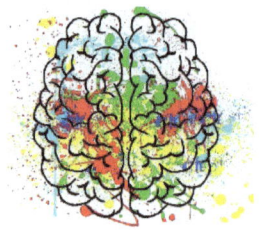

UNCAGED PSYCHOSIS
BOB MCNEIL

Often I wish beasts raised me,

as opposed to the parasites

who didn't get a therapist

after my body was used as a dartboard

by a half-brother who pricked innocence

until it was defiled repugnance.

Often I wish beasts raised me,

as opposed to the parasites

who didn't provide a CAT Scan

after my cranium was kicked

like a field goal by a-holes

with gridiron aggression.

Often I wish beasts raised me,

as opposed to the parasites

who let my mindset get

a zillion hallucinogen

that allowed my clouds

to be pulled in a tornado

of substance abuse

while I was a minor.

Often I wish I were an exterminator

with enough pesticide for each one of 'em.

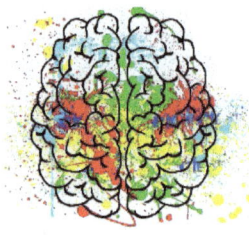

COMMUTING TO MYSELF
BOB MCNEIL

The fare to travel

this visceral subway

always goes up.

Commuting into myself

reveals train tracks

are my bones,

third rails

are my nerves,

and hungry rats

encapsulate my disposition.

Superego Transit Cops believe

my feelings could be anarchistic

underground cells,

so they check the bags

under my eyes,

considering if that's where

I keep my pipe bomb visions.

My ill-temper transfers

from train to train.

Sure enough,

my neuroses out gripes

sexagenarian grumblers

with each delay,

derelict aspirations panhandle

pleading to get some pleasure,

and my other big bipolar hordes

can't get their problems

through the exits.

The Inner Voice

Address System

apologizes for the traffic

up ahead.

It explains why

turtles in a tar pit

would be better at transporting

me to my destination.

Ever a philomath,

I inspect the transit map

and seek life's right station.

Maybe on the next ride,

I'll find it.

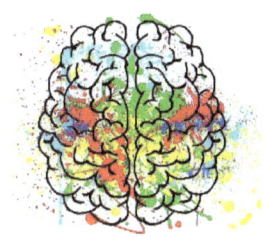

FOES

BOB MCNEIL

Staring at the computer screen, Ernesto Palabra considered an arctic scene in his story. He wondered if the character Andro-Toid X33 should use laser-emitting fans of war or arrow-launching armlets to defeat a skyscraper-tall ice monster. All descriptions about the 50-foot mechanical defender of mortals satiated his need for heroism. Something about having a genetically designed meta-intelligent human brain in an automaton appealed to him. Even the idea of it looking like a Samurai in blue-colored armor had great allure. Details about the arch-enemy, a humanoid-shaped mutation created by global warming, addressed the writer's didactic needs as well. Their battle continued in Ernesto's mind. It just needed a dénouement.

"Ernie, it's 3:00 in the morning. Are you coming to bed?" The sci-fi composer's girlfriend screamed from their bedroom.

"Yeah, yeah, I'll be there soon."

Something about his companion's screeching voice made Ernesto type faster. Torrential tapping noises filled the living room. Heavy-handedly, the logophile banged out more paragraphs about the war-waging duo on his laptop.

"Turn off the light and come to bed, man."

"OK, I will."

"Now damn it."

Right alongside remembered philistines and naysayers, the creature's head fell after the automaton shot out incendiary arrows from two extended arms. The vanquisher wanted to defeat other foes, but the writer fueling his existence turned off the computer. It was either that or verbally wrestle with another adversary on a Queen-sized bed.

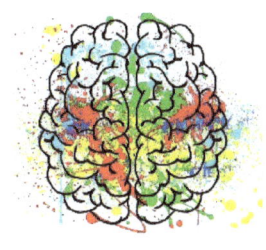

LOTTERY

JACK FREEDMAN

My mental health is a lottery
Stability is a daily game of chance

Unknown as to whether
This bingo cage will release
My exhausted survival skills
Or my self-destructive behavior

Eighty emotions contained in one heart
Six moods released from one brain

Shuffling like the wind
Inside a glass sphere

Sometimes spinning

Like a centrifuge

My precious energy is

Hyperactive and preparing

For an outburst

Of ear shattering screams

Too much pressure

To appear stable

After emotions

Are released

Every day is an act of gambling

Where I could experience

Combinations of simple emotions

Creating a complex

Inside a withered spirit

All these bouncing balls

Have the impact

Of my inner child

Jumping upon my back

Like an inflatable surface

At a birthday party

I'm getting too old

To appear stable to all

Who eventually get to know me

I do not fear violence from my enemies

I fear my mind far worse than any gangster

And my only supplemental number

Comes from the phone

From which I call the man

Who sells me weed

For sometimes

All it takes

To soothe me

Is a dime bag

And a lucid dream

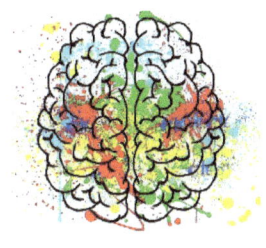

THE COLORS I HEAR
RENATA PAVREY

I see colors for sounds,

Taste shapes and hear textures

I recognize faces based on

Auditory rainbows -

Colors that the sounds produce

And not the voices themselves

Someone's screaming rivers of gushing aquamarine

Footsteps heavy like leaden rain-soaked clouds

Waiting to burst forth into my space;

I hear a cobalt blue voice

Green coils of smoke slither into my room

A chorus of ultramarine

Accompanies dusts of lilac and lavender;

Somewhere in the background

Icicles of blue crystals

Sparkle and glimmer with queries

Colors of conversations

Soak into the fabric of words

Bleed into each other

And present a palette of different hues;

A quilt of dialogue

That shows more than it tells;

They say silence is golden

But I see no color at all

When everything is quiet

Wrapped in a musical shawl

Shimmering colors transport me

To dance land, as the music plays -

A deep, glossy, crimson cello

The piano dazzles like a checkerboard

Rose and salmon spiral out from flute holes

Burnt sienna speaks from the guitar's core

A yellow triangle floating in space
Shows me it's the trumpet

Numbers and days have colors, too
Today is Monday
I know because it's orange
People talk about Monday blues
But I see Monday as a golden orange orb
Of possibilities and hopes
For the week ahead;
Three is a cheery lemon
Five is a vibrant coquelicot
But thirty-five is a depressing beige

Colors wash over me ambivalently
Truth radiates phosphorescence
Lies, hate and disappointment
Are darker than the blackest black;
We all perceive the world differently
Diversity can be a glorious thing
When you have a harlequin of hues to hear

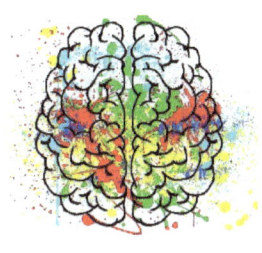

READING DIVERSITY
RENATA PAVREY

The members of Read The World Book Club always look forward to their monthly book discussions. They spend the entire month reading the chosen book—selected in turn by different members—and can't wait to present their thoughts and opinions at the eagerly awaited literary curation of ideas. The book picked for the month of June was *The Reason I Jump* by Naoki Higashida. Originally written in Japanese, the memoir has been translated into English by David Mitchell (popularly known for *Cloud Atlas* and *Slade House*, among other well known works). Priya had picked the title this month, because the book club was keen on discussing a non-fiction book. They had been reading a lot of translated fiction from classic and contemporary writers in the past few months, and were looking for something new and different to talk about.

The meeting has been scheduled at Sam's place today, the last Sunday of the month (when all their book meets occur, to give everyone sufficient time to finish the book). Sam starts off by commending Priya on her choice of book for the month. "It was nothing like I expected," he informs her and everyone else. "I, too, wasn't aware that the writer was a thirteen-year-old boy with autism when I picked up this book," Priya admits. "A Japanese language memoir sounded interesting, and it was David Mitchell's name on the cover (as translator) that caught my attention." "We learned so much," shares Geneve. *"The Reason I Jump* is certainly a one-of-a-kind memoir that showcases how an autistic mind thinks and perceives. I hadn't known much about autism earlier, because I personally don't know anyone with autism. I've heard about it as a spectrum disorder, but until reading Naoki's book I had no experience with people with autism."

Many of the book club members reiterate Priya's and Geneve's thoughts. They dove into the book expecting something else and came out with insights and information like never before. Using an alphabet grid to construct words and sentences, the child author writes about his life with autism in a neurotypical world, and answers questions that people don't have answers to, or never knew they needed to ask in the first place. Why do people with autism repeat words and phrases, why do they line up blocks and toys, why do they avoid eye contact, why do they jump and flap their arms???? Questions upon questions from non-autistic minds, unanswered until now, or never asked before because they did not consider minds different from their own.

Naoki Higashida was diagnosed with autism at age 5, wrote the Japanese book at age 13, and the English translation came out eight years later by British author

David Mitchell, whose own child is autistic. Mitchell translated the book because he wanted to help others like himself and his wife—parents, siblings, teachers, caregivers—to understand and support their loved ones on the spectrum. Naoki's honesty and generosity provide unique insights into not only his life with autism, but on autism as a whole and life itself. In teaching us to understand others, it helps us understand ourselves and our role in fostering better relationships in society. Written in the form of Q & As, the illuminating narrative structure is just like Naoki's alphabet grid—understanding and empathizing with autistic behaviors that are communicated through so much more than words.

Like many people on the spectrum, Naoki has speech difficulties, but his story is a revelatory account of autism, beautifully translated onto the page in his own words and language. One of the book club members, Lata, points out that after reading the book she started looking up other literature written by or about autism spectrum disorders. "I came across the word neurodivergency and began reading up on it. *Autism in Heels* by Jennifer O'Toole was another book I read alongside *The Reason I Jump*," Lata reveals. "The memoir is about the author's journey of being diagnosed with Asperger's Syndrome at the age of 35, and presents a firsthand account of autism in women." Lata appreciated the insights she gained from both books, written across different ages and genders, and learning how wide and misunderstood the spectrum can be.

Like Lata, other members also researched books on autism when they realized how little they knew on the subject. More book recommendations started pouring forth—*At Home in the Land of Oz* by Anne Clinard Barnhill (the writer's memoir of living with her autistic sister), *Animals in Translation* by Temple Grandin (an animal behaviour expert with autism talking about the autistic brain and the human-animal bond), *The Color of Bee Larkham's Murder* by Sarah J. Harris (the protagonist is a child on the spectrum who witnesses a murder), *The Curious Incident of the Dog in the Night-time* by Mark Haddon (a teenager with Asperger's Syndrome out to solve the murder of the neighbour's dog), *Odd Girl Out* by Laura James (an autistic mom raising non-autistic children talks about the under-diagnosis of female autism), *How Can I Talk If My Lips Don't Move* by Tito Rajarshi Mukhopadhyay (a non-verbal autistic who finds expression in reading and writing) —an assortment of books on autism spectrum disorders across fiction and non-fiction, with a range of autistic characters in prominent roles.

As the list grew, the Read the World Book Club members realized that they were not as widely read as they had imagined. They had undoubtedly read a lot of books, but their reading habits were not diversified. Their reading choices were not inclusive of authors, characters and situations different from their own. By making a conscious effort to venture out of mainstream authors and popular bestsellers, they learned to appreciate the vastness of literature and its many forms. They learned how books can be educational and not just entertaining. They learned to look beyond their own lives and see and know human beings for who they are. They learned to appreciate the interconnectedness of humanity and what makes us human.

Armed with their list of new titles to read, Sam concludes the book meeting with plans to ensure that their reading is more diverse from now on. "I, for one, am going to read Naoki Higashida's follow-up book next," Nick states, while alluding to *Fall Down 7 Times Get Up 8* – a sequel to *The Reason I Jump* that Naoki wrote at age 24. "What book on neurodivergency are you going to pick up next?"

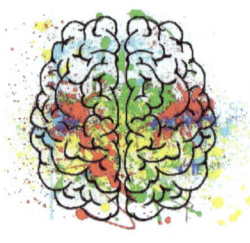

SHOWDOWN

IVAN DRAGO

"But who would love a broken person? You're nothing but damaged goods. You're pathetic, broken, useless. They will all leave you, especially Her."

Heh

"That's where you're wrong. Her and I have a bond stronger than ever, stronger than what you've ever known, while you're nothing but a vile Daemon."

"So naïve. Perhaps I should teach you a lesson."

Well shit

The Daemon draws out her weapons, eager to draw blood

"A lesson in futility, perhaps."

No backing down now, I suppose

As I draw my bladed chains, I know I stand no chance on winning this fight. But I figure might as well make this count.

"So be it."

Please give me the strength to defeat and destroy this Daemon, O Priestess.

As we both charge, I know for sure that one of us is walking out of here alive, or we're both dying.

I can't fail this; I can't fail Her.

I need to win this, I need to do this

For Her

Her...

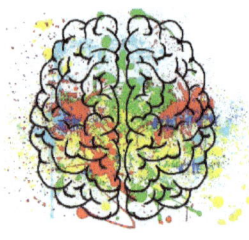

BLACKNESS

IVAN DRAGO

Chained…

Locked…

Trapped…

Nowhere to go…

Stuck in this hell…

No escape…

No freedom…

Stuck alone…

No hope…

Only despair…

Sanity eroding…

I pray…

Pray for my suffering to end…

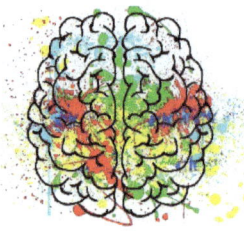

HOLE

IVAN DRAGO

There's a hole in my chest

Where a heart used to be

I gave it to someone

Only for it to be broken

Each day I cry

Each day I'm sad

Each day I want her back

But I can't

Because she found someone

Now, there is a hole in my chest

Where a heart used to be

It is empty

Like me

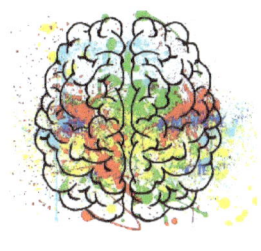

UNTITLED

AMY PENNEY

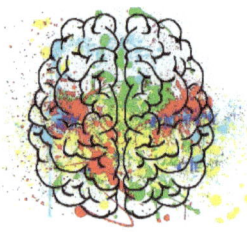

UNTITLED
AMY PENNEY

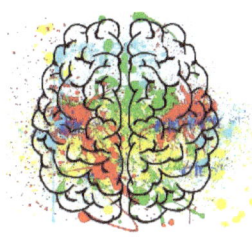

UNTITLED
AMY PENNEY

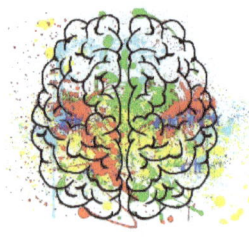

UNTITLED
AMY PENNEY

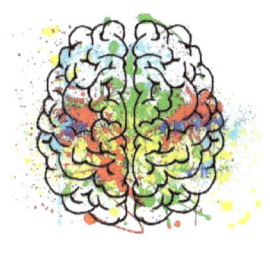

UNTITLED
AMY PENNEY

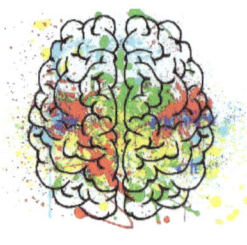

UNTITLED
AMY PENNEY

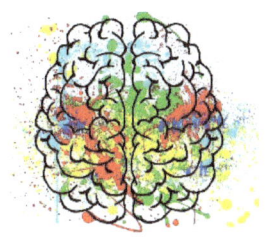

UNTITLED

AMY PENNEY

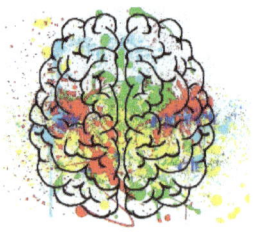

UNTITLED
AMY PENNEY

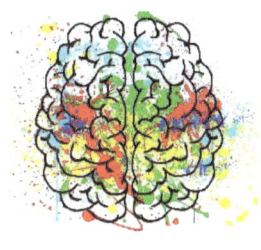

UNTITLED
AMY PENNEY

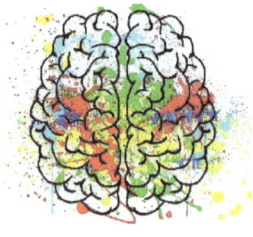

UNTITLED
AMY PENNEEY

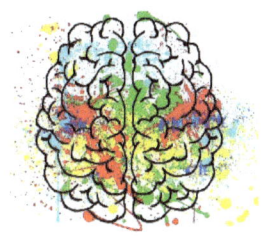

UNTITLED
AMY PENNEY

burst out of myself
into the river held back
too long

i am in it though it is me
rushing forward and through

swift and cool redemption

my heart so far ahead
beating with
such
flutter and fever

a starling leaving its nest

i now allow my current:

carry me onward to
where birds always fly

my heart
so far beyond the horizon
above churning waters of
my
own
making

to the endless
of boundaries no more

and settle easy on banks
of a life

just

begun

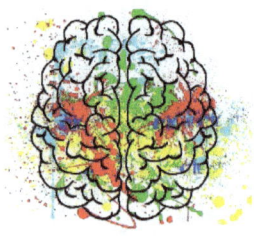

UNTITLED
AMY PENNEY

it is in these late hours i am in restless rest
 feel lungs in their function;

joints that remain still and those that persist in their
movement
 the muscles surrounding that ache

the body is a heavy thing to move when the operator is
dead

put both hands on your head

and

feel the shape of your

scull

you'd be surprised

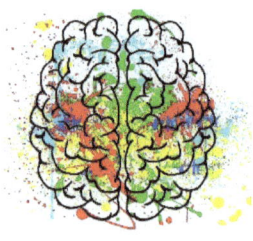

UNTITLED
AMY PENNEY

so came the slip of cold spring through my gums

my shudder at the glimpse of its cut and churning

no mistake of winter here

green promises keep theirs under grey skies that promise

see now how soft the groundwork lies after the cold

the upheaval of dark season to bright

pure color

the chutes of the months to come so sweet

so long the quiet wait

the haze of birds chirping

the hoof prints in the muddied yard, pointed toward the apple tree

fog that soothes the lungs so calm like the color blue

how the woods smell

the earth so soft and so quiet are these days of waiting for the time

though no absolute time

my waiting heart could break in sun flakes at the thought of it all

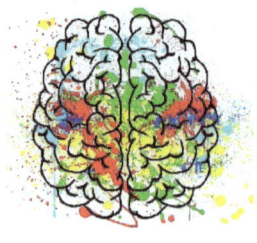

UNTITLED
AMY PENNEY

sprawl of intake

recoil of remain

leak,

slow digression into my veins

and draw me closer to those who knew me

when geometry was a big deal

the chalk on the boards

the dust

rush like pearl to the nightstand and rain only beneath

the light of totality

this blade no longer rests on the tarmac

...individual cadence...

stay with me now

we are going down

the resolve of history which defines has sunk too low to
dredge

the world is boundary shaken

the safe transgression in my colleague of sorts; the mind so
divine

so tailored for me and my doings about the world

how the people i have known would play such part to hold
our hands together and

feel how time has changed our palms

but to know now we were once a band of loved ones

then, yet unaware

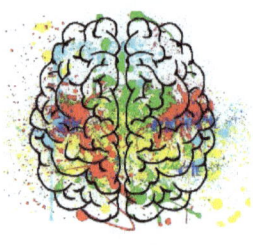

UNTITLED
AMY PENNEY

The slow implosion of things settles in
a place unknown to most
below my ribcage

center

A sandbag of my life fills and fills and
fills
and here I choke at the fullness

and

don't the bones have such structure
when i can feel

the imagined beneath them

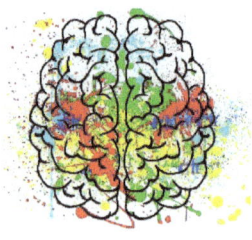

UNTITLED
AMY PENNEY

Call on me now in the crest of this day

mind welling at the call of some bird who

reminds me that somewhere there is wholeness in me

a place far removed for goodness' sake

Rest your feet upon the wreckage of my winter branches
and

weave your nest within its creaking joints

I could be quite alive in the symphony of evening

should a song be sung from nature's swell

Leave me at rest with my roots
there is water enough

sprawl, instead, with the likeliness of life from my spread
tend, though, the gentle of life revealing

I have a life that no one has seen

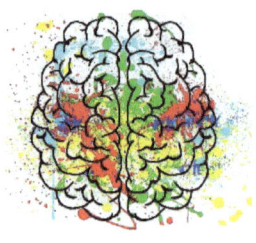

UNTITLED
AMY PENNEY

The canned sigh

lends me to heave what is left back at it

I am sickened by the prospect of the day after the

day after the day

lugging baggage like a woodpile on my back

I am shrug on the pavement in summer

I am sway in the lunge of winter

No further will i guide my breath for

the autumn and spring of its settle

The world only hurts so much while its dreaming

The direction from here

from now

awaits its juror

If not me

it must be me

What is it i have been waiting for and

What was i

expecting

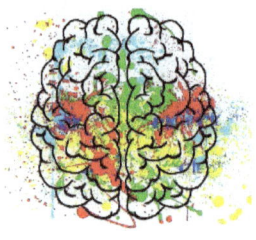

DARK IMAGINATION

MAGNOLIA SILCOX

Some say I have what you call a bit of an overactive imagination. However, it's not my fault that I see Cthulhu trying to turn my cat into one of his evil minions. My name is Magnolia Silcox and I have Schizophrenia.

From early on in my life I could always see things that weren't there. I would see blue little dots on my walls when I was about eight and I would call them angels. I had an alligator named Marfa that would talk and snap at things. Her tail would fall off and then magically grow back.

Some people might say that these are just childish things, and most people outgrow them when they are older. But the thing about me is that I never outgrew these things like most people do. I have too many imaginary friends and enemies that seem to follow me everywhere.

When I was fourteen, I started to see more things that other people couldn't see. Only these ones were much darker and graphic. They also looked more realistic and much more vivid. The first thing I saw was blood covering my hands. It was pouring out everywhere. I tried to make it stop but yet it wouldn't. No matter how hard I tried to get the blood off of me it wouldn't come off.

Over the next few days things started to get worse. I saw my friends covered in blood saying that they weren't my real friends. This terrified the shit out of me. But I just hoped that no one would notice what was happening to me. Unfortunately, I couldn't keep this secret of mine hidden from the world forever.

One night I could feel cockroaches crawling up and down my skin. I could see their ugly poop brown bodies. I was covered in them from head to toe. I then started crying and scratching at my skin. I wanted them off my body. My dad then heard me crying and ran into my room.

"What's wrong?" he asked.

"The bugs are all over me and I can't get them off." I cried.

My mom then came in and suggested I take a bath and change my clothes. When I got out, I could hear them talking about me downstairs.

"I think we need to go find her a psychiatrist or get her in to see someone." my mom explained.

"I think she's crazy." I heard my dad whisper.

That was a time I felt deeply hurt by my parents in a way that I can't really explain. If there's one thing I hate more than anything it's people calling me crazy. Thing is

I'm nowhere close to being a crazy person. I don't sacrifice kittens to the devil. I don't kidnap babies and hold them hostage. I don't sell drugs to the cartel. I'm just a normal person with a couple of extra issues that I have to deal with.

My dad spent months and months trying to find a special kind of doctor that would see me but yet it was to no avail. All of them were full of patients and none were willing to accept me.

Things at school became harder for me. I had trouble focusing on my work. The demons in the corner scared the hell out of me. They would follow me everywhere and no matter what I could never get rid of them. There were these furry little black monsters that would whisper things in a language that I couldn't understand. I could see clouds of darkness and light hovering over people. Demons would be attached to them and would tell them to do horrible things.

When people ask me to describe Schizophrenia I would say that it is like hell on earth. It's like a nightmare that you can never wake up from. You are stuck in the plot of a horror movie and no matter how hard you try you can never escape the monsters. The experience is different for everyone but for me I am trapped in a hell of my mind's own making.

High School is a time of finding yourself and well I was finding out some things about myself that were a bit uncomfortable and embarrassing. I realized how hot women were. That I was attracted to them in a sexual way.

For a girl coming from a very conservative Christian background, I didn't really know how to confront these feelings.

I got bullied a lot in the locker room for having homosexual feelings. The other girls would laugh at me and mock me. I had many people from my Bible Club who I thought would be there for me saying that I was living in sin.

Thing is what made it a million times worse is I would hear voices saying vulgar things about me. They told me that I was worthless and that I should just end it all. How I would be better off dead.

I started to listen to them and that is when my suicide attempts began. I would try to cut my skin with a razor and drown myself in the tub. I kept thinking about more and more ways to kill myself.

I had my final break when I went to this Christian youth group with my friend. The girls made fun of me there for liking girls. When I went home that day my mom noticed something wasn't quite right with me. I seemed a bit off.

The next day I was looking at my phone and crying. My mom then took the phone from me so I got in my flip flops and ran out the door.

I didn't know where to go or what to do but I figured my parents would abandon me if they found out the truth about my sexuality.

I ran down the street in my flip flops crying. I figured that this was now the perfect time to kill myself. I had been running for hours and hours. I didn't know what time of night that it was. My feet had huge blisters all over them. I was dehydrated and out of breath. I tried asking people for a phone to use so I could get some help but no one would help me.

Eventually I found this apartment complex. There was a lady who pulled up to the side of the road.

"Do you need help sweetie?" she asked me.

"Yes." I answered.

Her niece then opened the car door and let me inside. I sat in her house for a while. I ate some watermelon and drank lots of water. I was there until she called the cops.

They then asked me a bunch of simple questions like what the year was and where I was. But even those simple questions were hard for me to answer. I learned that whenever I'm stressed out my speech becomes incoherent, and nobody understands what I am saying. My thoughts seem to blur together, and everything becomes a bit hazy.

They hooked me up to a bunch of things to check my heart rate and things like that. At first, they thought I was high on some type of drug but then they figured out that I had a heart problem that caused it to beat faster than normal.

I was then allowed to sit in the back of the cop car.

"Why did you run away from home?" he asked me.

"I thought my parents wouldn't want me because I like girls." I replied.

"Hey, we all feel rejected by our parents at some point. I was raised in a Mormon household. My parents thought I'd have lots of kids. But me and my wife never wanted that many kids." he explained.

That made me feel a bit better about myself. At least I wasn't the only one that felt they didn't live up to their parents' standards. By the time his story was over I was then rushed to an ambulance. I was put on this long hospital bed. The guy asked me the same questions as the cop. I then repeated my story.

"We had a woman like you just the other day. She was in a relationship with another woman. But she tried to kill herself because she thought her future mother-in-law wouldn't accept their relationship. I have many friends who are homosexual. Anyone who abandons someone for something like that is a bad person." he explained.

The ambulance guy then gave me a bottle to drink and said he wouldn't stick any needles in me if I drank that bottle of water. So I drank it and he asked me some questions.

We then arrived at the hospital and I was taken inside. The doctors stuck a bunch of needles inside of me and hooked me up to a bunch of IVs. I was in bed for hours just staring at the hospital walls

Hours later my parents finally rushed into the building. The staff asked if I wanted to see them and I said that it would be alright.

My mom came into the hospital room crying.

"I love you no matter what Magnolia." she admitted.

She then pulled out her phone and said that my dad was waiting in the lobby and wanted to get in touch with me.

"Hey, Magnolia, I love you no matter what ok?" my dad cried.

That was the first time I had ever heard my dad cry and break down into tears. In fact, it's been the only time I've ever seen him cry to that extent.

After my parents left I was then sent to an ambulance. That's where I learned for the first time that people can imprison you for attempting suicide. They don't necessarily call it that but that's what it is more or less. I was on a police hold for one week. Meaning I was forced to stay in a mental institution for an entire week.

When I arrived at the mental institution they searched me up and down for any scars and illegal items. I was then sent back and given breakfast. It was all cold but yet it was still something to eat.

My mom was there and she was given a list of all the activities and therapy things I would be doing. I later learned that the entire schedule was a load of bullshit. We never actually did any of the activities listed there. It was all just a scam to make the place look better for the families that put their family members in there.

When my mom left and I was sent back to the children's and teen's ward I was scared. I didn't know how long I would be there or what was going to happen to me. I felt trapped and there was no way that I could escape. I kept pacing back and forth through the halls. That's what most people do in mental institutions after they slowly begin to lose their sanity. They just walk back and forth through the halls. Mental institutions do little to help the people there; they just keep them there until they've received enough money from the state and then they dump them back on the streets.

While I was there for an entire week, I went through traumatic experiences that only made my mental state worse. I saw teenagers yell at one another and beat each other up. They pulled each other's clothes to shreds and pulled one another's hair out. The staff did little to keep us safe.

I had terrible hallucinations that kept me up at night. There was a pale gray man with sharp fangs tossing an apple back and forth in his hands. But that wasn't even the most terrifying hallucination that I had. There was a girl that looked exactly like me, only she was completely dead. She had black goo oozing out of her eyes. Maggots were swarming all over her. She had gray skin that was rotting and peeling off. It creeped me the hell out seeing someone that looked exactly like me except she was dead and decaying.

There were mean people in that mental institution that I hope to never meet again. My roommate that sexually assaulted me and I was still forced to share a room with her after that incident. As well as the girl who threatened to kill me.

"You keep looking at me and I'll kill you." she muttered under her breath at me.

That scared me of the fact that this girl much bigger and taller than me was threatening to kill me. Even though I wasn't staring at her at all. I was just out of it staring at hallucinations over in the corner.

I was a scared and terrified kid that didn't know what to do. I didn't want to fight anyone either because there's this thing in mental institutions called booty juice. The staff takes a big shot and sticks it in your butt then it paralyzes you immediately. Those shots have always scared me and I never want to get one.

The rest of my stay was just abysmal with nothing really happening. The medication they put me on messed with my head. I felt slow and dumb as though it took me a million years to accomplish simple things.

The only way to get out of that hellhole was to lie your way out of the system. I learned how to lie on my suicidal behavioral sheets just to get out of there. They make those sheets extremely easy to lie on. You basically lie that you're completely happy and that you have no thoughts about killing yourself or others. Even though that couldn't be farther from the truth. That place only made me more depressed and I wanted to only kill myself more. The truth is that everybody lies on those tests because almost any place is better than a mental institution.

When I finally got out of that horrible place it was then time to go back to school. At school things only got harder for me. I couldn't keep up with the workload that the magnet program had placed one me. The medication caused me to do things that I would normally never do. They made me extremely tired to the point where I would fall asleep in the middle of class.

My teacher had to wake me up several times but I just kept falling asleep over and over again. He made me stay after class to ask me some questions. When I explained to him that I was on antipsychotics he looked at me like I had just murdered someone.

I kept missing days of school to go see a psychologist that played weird sort of games with me and wrote notes about it. He showed me different abstract drawings and asked me to describe what I was seeing.

After weeks of doing tests he finally diagnosed me with pre-formed Schizophrenia. I had Schizophrenia but yet it wasn't severe to the point where I was unable to do anything.

I tried my best to make it through the school year but yet I kept having problems. Sometimes my episodes would get really bad that I would go to the nurse and tell her I was hallucinating. She always seemed to get mad at me because she thought that I was doing drugs and getting high. But I explained everything to her. She then called up my parents and my dad came to her office.

"She should be put up in a mental institution. Or stay home and we can have a teacher come and see her. I'm afraid she's a danger to other students." the counselor explained.

I wondered how I could be a danger to other students. I was a straight A student in the Honors classes. I did my best to be a perfect student and excel in school. I wasn't a threat or a menace to anyone.

The thing is when you have Schizophrenia it doesn't matter what you do people will always treat you like a monster. They treat you like you are a deranged killer on the loose that's ready to pull a knife on someone at any second. I mostly blame the media for these horrible stereotypes. The crime shows show murderers that kill people because of the voices in their head. The news which shows people having psychotic breakdowns and going on killing sprees. Schizophrenic people are almost always never shown in a positive light or shown doing normal things like getting married or having kids.

Sometimes I think the stigma is worse than the hallucinations and delusions themselves. I hate being treated like a monster when I have done nothing wrong.

Bible Club was one of the only places I felt safe and happy. That is until I met this strange man. I asked people to pray for me because I was having trouble with my hallucinations. Then he came up to me and said that I had a spiritual gift.

This man had a very inappropriate relationship with me that made me feel uncomfortable. He kept saying odd things like how I was meant to marry him and have sex with him even though he was much older than me. He told me that I should get rid of my medication because they had demons in them.

I was out of it for most of the time since I wasn't on my medication. But something didn't sit well when his mom told me to go to Panama with them and to not tell my parents.

I told my parents, and they called the cops. Turns out that man ran a cult in Panama that did horrible things to children. Unspeakable and evil things to innocent people. One of their leaders told a boy to cut off his toe and feed it to a snake so that he'd get closer to God.

Senior year things went pretty well for me and I met some new people at a different school. I hung out with this guy at lunch and we eventually started dating.

COVID hit and then everything got crazy. I spent a lot of time at my boyfriend's house to escape everything. All the places in Las Vegas were closed including the strip. My dad was in a different state and the stores were running out of groceries.

At the time I thought my boyfriend was going to be there for me forever. He promised me that he would never leave me and that he'd marry me someday. We stayed together for three years. His mom let me visit him several times. But something was up with him and I found out about it little by little. He would look at pictures of naked girls on his phone and I would see texts of other girls calling him hot or sexy. He claimed they were just his friends but I knew better than that. He would get really defensive whenever I looked over at his phone.

Things started to get worse when I stayed over at his house for a month. He would yell and cuss at me every day. When I accused him of cheating, he would always get really defensive and angry at me. His room was absolutely disgusting. He had rotten food and dirty dishes all over the place. I got tired of it always looking like that, so I decided to clean it up one day. He then got angry and started arguing with me over the fact that I cleaned his room. I would want to cuddle with him and then he would get angry at me because I was interrupting his gaming time. I was also apparently interrupting the time he had with his friends.

All his yelling and fighting with me caused me to stress out. I was hallucinating even more than I normally was. I felt depressed and suicidal because nothing I ever did could make him happy or please him. It got so bad to the point where his mom even noticed and asked if I needed to go home.

My boyfriend said things that made me uncomfortable. He said that I'm not really good at anything other than writing and that I could be a great porn star. I was enraged at him when he said that. I explained to him that I never wanted to be a porn star. But yet he would talk about it often and I just wanted him to shut the hell up. I have nothing against people who choose that for their career but it's not a career path that I would ever choose.

Eventually I had my breaking point when we got into a huge argument. The voices then told me how I'm worthless and that I should just end my miserable existence. So, I listened to them and took a bunch of pills.

I then began convulsing and shaking like crazy. His mom then called the cops and paramedics, and I was then rushed to the hospital. My blood pressure was low and I was given several needles and IVs. After being in the hospital for a day I was then sent to yet another mental institution.

While I was in the mental institution I panicked but it was the thought that my boyfriend still loved me that kept me going. It was hard for me to get in touch with him but I was finally able to.

"I'm sorry we're breaking up." he answered.

"No, please don't." I cried.

"I'm sorry," he stated.

He then hung up on me and I broke down into tears. Even the staff member that let me borrow his phone looked saddened. I just laid in my bed the entire day crying and crying until I could no longer cry.

My dad eventually got a hold of me through the front desk phone. He told me that if I ever wanted to get out of there I needed to stop crying and pretend to be happy. He told me that he would do his best to bail me out there. That he was sorry about what happened between me and my boyfriend.

So as heartbroken as I was, I pretended that I had just won a trip to the Bahamas. I pretended to be the happiest person in the world. I went to all their dumb programs and filled out all their stupid smiley face sheets.

My dad then got up at 2 am in the morning and drove an entire day to come and pick me up. He got absolutely no sleep in order to pick me up on time. I am thankful he came to bail me out of there.

The day I got out my ex-boyfriend blew up my phone and wouldn't stop messaging me. But I didn't care to get back with him. Why would I want to be with someone that left me when I desperately needed him the most? If he couldn't be there for me when I attempted suicide then he didn't deserve to be a part of my life anymore.

My dad told me that I should just block him. So, I did even though it was hard.

"When I went over to their house to go get your stuff, he was over at a friend's house. He wasn't there worried about you and hoping you were ok. He doesn't care about you. I asked his mom about you, and she said that he didn't want to be with you because he thought you were too clingy and attached to him. If he can't suck it up and put your needs before his then he's not a real man. He's not ready to be in a committed relationship." my dad explained.

It hurt but yet I knew he was right. All this time I thought my boyfriend would be worried about me to some extent but he didn't even care about me. His mom seemed more worried about me; she even called me on my dad's phone and asked if I was ok. It hurt me deeply to know that he didn't even give a single damn about me. I was nothing more than a side piece and a hot piece of ass to him.

I tried to move on from him but it was hard. I spent weeks doing nothing but crying in my bed. My mom took me out to buy new clothes to cheer me up. She reassured me that karma would eventually find him and bite him in the butt.

Even though I kept blocking him he still found ways to contact me. One day he'd say things like how he still loves me and wants me in his life. The next day he'd say things like how I'm going to turn out to be a bitch like my mother and that I am going to die alone. That I'm a bad person and I'm toxic for him.

I let these stupid words get to my head and it would ruin my whole day and cause me to bawl my eyes out.

All those things that he had once said to me had been flushed down the drain. He made up this fantasy that I would be a famous author and he would be this famous boxer making millions. All that was now gone, and I felt so lost.

I guess what my mom had told me was right. Karma did eventually come for my ex though. He messaged me one day saying he wanted to be friends. So, I played along with his little game. I asked him how his boxing was going, and he said that he had given up on that. All those years he had talked about being a boxer and he had given up on it because he thought it was too hard. But yet here I was still standing victorious and accomplishing my goals of becoming an author. So I blocked him like he had done to me several times and that's the last I heard from him.

Truth be told, I am still a bit lonely. It would be nice to have a significant other in my life to support me when the hallucinations get bad. But I don't need some prince charming to come and save me from a tower. I can climb out of the tower on my own just fine. This queen doesn't need a king. I can rule my world just fine on my own.

After a couple of months, I got a job working at a prison. The days were long and hard. I was not given any training as to how to deal with inmates and I was scared and alone. It was alright though because they at least paid well. Working there for eight hours was fine even though the swing shift got to me.

But then they started to make me work fifteen- and sixteen-hour days. My hallucinations got worse and worse with the added stress. I wasn't able to get enough sleep at night and it left me feeling tired at work. Working with the women inmates was bad enough I'd get several of them yelling and cussing at me. But the men were even worse than the women. They looked at me like I was a juicy piece of meat. The inmates would ask weird requests of me all the time. They asked me to bring in beer and cigarettes. They offered me jobs like to be there to look out when they went to order crack. But I told them to fuck off and that I wasn't going to do shit for them.

Nothing good ever happened there and there were scary instances that happened. One girl killed herself and hung herself in her cell. Another tried to pour chemicals all over herself and kill herself. They kept trying to steal food from the kitchen and they hid it in every crack and crevice of their body you can think of. So I had to throw away food that was shoved up their junk and report it to the correctional officers. Fights broke out almost every single week. One even broke out in the cafeteria. Two girls started throwing food at each other and beating each other up. One girl tried to start a riot in the cafeteria because my co-worker refused to make peanut butter packets to go with the inmate's meals. The dog that would sniff out drugs came around to search for drugs. The women would take the fruit we gave out at meals and would make contraband alcohol in their toilets.

While I thought that the inmates were bad, my co-workers refused to give me a lunch break. They refused to help me clean up the place so that it would pass a health inspection.

Things got worse when my boss had the grand idea that the men's prison would cook for us. The men would send us food that was either burnt or raw. So, the women would have to cook it.

My hallucinations got really bad, and they told me horrible things. They told me to stick a thermometer in my eyes and gouge them out. Once there was a thunderstorm inside the kitchen and it felt like it was raining. I was about to reach my breaking point working in such a stressful environment with zero support and training.

One day I was called into an office to talk to the warden of the prison. She told me that I was being too kind to the inmates and telling them things they shouldn't know. That she was going to have me removed. I explained to her that I wasn't telling the inmates personal things like my address or names of my family members because I didn't want them to find me. But I was given zero training to know how to deal with them so how was I supposed to know? She said that it was my fault that they were asking me for things like alcohol and cigarettes. But I disagree completely. They asked all of my co-workers for inappropriate things. The men asked my female co-worker to have sex with them even though she refused. The woman asked her for cigarettes and alcohol as well so I didn't understand why this would pertain exclusively to me.

As for sharing personal information I wasn't telling them anything like my phone number, address, names of family members, where I lived. Nothing of the sort. In fact, my boss and my other co-workers were sharing what the warden was considering personal information. One of my co-workers talked about his trip to Mexico, his wife, and owning a taco truck. Another one of my coworkers talked about her fiancé. My boss would talk about her child with special needs and how it was difficult for her to deal with the kid. Even the cops would talk about their favorite sports teams and other jobs they used to have around the prisoners.

So, I call bullshit. What the warden was really doing was singling me out because she knew I was different. She had found out that I had a disability, and she was doing whatever she could to get rid of me. So, I decided to quit as I didn't really care to work fifteen to sixteen hours a day without a lunch break. As well as only one day off sometimes.

So, I guess that's my story of living with Schizophrenia. The world has thrown a lot of stuff my way but yet I'm still standing. I'm still alive and well. I have a family that loves me, as well as a dog. I am able to write and be a published author. I am able to travel around the country and visit new places. I am thankful for the things I am able to do in my life. I know that some are not as fortunate.

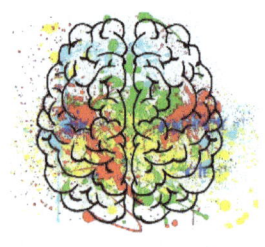

CONCENTRATION OR BUST: HOW THE PILATES SYSTEM STRENGTHENED ME INSIDE AND OUT

MELISSA GREENWOOD

There's an exercise in Pilates called "coordination," and when my clients are about to transition into it, having just finished their frog and leg circles, I can literally see them thinking through the steps in their heads: curl up off of the Reformer with knees and elbows bent at 90 degrees; extend the arms and legs out simultaneously; open/close the legs, carriage-width; bend the knees back in first, while reaching the arms out longer still; bend the elbows in last—maintaining the lift and abdominal scoop. It's an exercise that is harder mentally than it is physically, and it perfectly captures the spirit of *concentration*—one of the six principles of Pilates (the other five include control, centering, precision, breath, and flow). Completing the exercise correctly can feel like patting your head while rubbing your belly or like playing a round of the aptly-named Concentration game, a sleep-away camp favorite: *Concentration, concentration is the game. Keep the rhythm. Keep the rhythm just the same. Subject: Pilates.* Meanwhile, we'd be slap-slapping our knees, then snap-snapping our fingers, first on our right hand and then on our left.

All my life, I excelled in school despite not having natural abilities in most subjects (I was unathletic, a poor speller, bad at math, confused in science, and geographically- and directionally-challenged) because, unlike my younger brother, who had an official ADHD-diagnosis, I could readily concentrate. A strong writer with equally-strong focus, I could whip out a five- or ten-pager in college on the night before it was due, and I often did. I didn't need to make an outline in advance to clarify my thoughts because my thoughts were crystalized on the page. Like Joan Didion, "I write entirely to find out what I'm thinking." I didn't even need Ritalin—like some of my peers were popping, often without prescription—to make my brain cooperate. *Concentration, concentration was the game.* And I was good at it.

Now, that's not to say that I was immune from distraction. In fact, when taking tests in high school, I would often turn my desk to the wall because seeing legs shaking—an annoying habit practiced by many of my classmates—distressed me. The repetitive movement, which I could spy out of the corner of my eyes, even from great distances away, reminded me of my hyperactive brother and irritated the crap out of me. When I got home, and it was time to do homework, I'd plead with my family to keep it down. "Be quiet," I'd yell from upstairs. "I can't hear myself think!" It's safe to say that I've always done my best focusing when the environment is "just so." But assuming the conditions were right, I could get my work done without a problem. There was no social media yet, and cell phones were *just for emergencies*—something my parents remind me of whenever they received a bill suggesting otherwise. By my 20s, even with a more habitual flip-phone habit and the advent of Myspace and Facebook, I could still focus when it counted—under pressure or for school and work deadlines.

***

Enter my dream role: communications manager for a K-8 school. By then, at 32 years old, I'd already sailed through college and graduate school, and I had the framed MFA degree to prove it. I'd earned multiple teaching credentials. I'd lived in two countries. I'd held down other jobs (albeit with limited success). And now, I even had a long-term boyfriend—my future-husband. I felt like my life was coming together, and now this position would be my first serious gig, paying a living wage with real benefits, and responsibilities. It sounded ideal, but I crumbled under the pressure like a thin sheet of paper under a too-heavy paperweight. My coworker, the school's technology director, found me in my office one day, shaking.

"Honey, what's the matter?" she asked, popping her head in. I had the door propped open for some ventilation in what was a windowless building. Dyvar was the resident mom—she addressed most of us with terms of endearment.

"Nothing. I'm just working," I said, barely looking up from my computer screen to acknowledge her. "I'm so behind." I'd been staying at the office until the custodial staff kicked me out every night at 10 pm, and I still couldn't keep up. I had Post-its glued to every inch of my desk—pink, purple, neon green, and highlighter yellow—but putting sticky notes everywhere and responding to each email and call on the fly—the organizational system that had worked for me in the past—wasn't working now. My energy was frenetic, my process chaotic and ineffectual. I kept interrupting one task to start another, then getting flustered when I couldn't remember where I'd left off or which deadline was the most pressing. One time, in my frenzy, I'd sent out an email to our stakeholders with the subject—"how is this?"—the very subject I had used when first okaying the content with my superior.

"You're shaking, dear."

"Oh, yeah. I've always had a bit of a tremor," I said unphased, letting out an uncomfortable squeal instead of the casual laugh I was aiming for. "Or maybe I'm just over-caffeinated?" I offered. At mid-afternoon, it *had* already been a two-cup day.

"Melissa, something's not right," Dyvar insisted—stepping closer. I think we should get you some herbal tea and take a little breather."

A few hours later, I was at urgent care, sent home with a note that excused me from work for the next three days on account of "exhaustion." That explained the awkward laughter and the shaking, which comforted me on some level: there was a physiological reason behind my behavior. Still, I really didn't want to accept the doctor's note, or his findings. *I have too much to do to rest,* I argued with as much gusto as I could muster, which wasn't much on account of the legitimate exhaustion. The physician, a gentle man, kept pressing, until I finally acquiesced and took the note from his hands. *I'll think about it,* I promised, knowing I wasn't going to win this argument. He smiled up at me softly from his swivel stool as if to say, "Attagirl." But the thought of forced-rest made me cringe. I'm a go-go-go kind of gal. I only nap when I have the flu, and, thanks to face masks, it's been a while. Yet, here was a man, a warm one who made me feel at ease and less ashamed for my abject failure—screwing up royally at my first "big girl" job, as I then called it—and he was telling me, in as kind a way as possible, that I might as well have had the flu and that I had to take it easy. He insisted.

Back at the office three days later, my bosses were also insistent—that I see a psychiatrist for what they believed was adult ADD, even though "we're not here to diagnose." I'm sure none of this was legal—perhaps part of the reason that, a few months later, they had me sign a document saying I wouldn't sue them, post-termination. (They sent me home for good on Election Day, 2016—also my then-fiancé's 30th birthday—with a $3,000 severance check and a crushed self-image. Later that day, Trump won the election.) But, before that shitshow of a November 8th, I did as they asked. I made an appointment with an in-network doctor who, prior to our appointment, had me order a book off of Amazon. The book took the reader through a checklist to determine whether she might have adult ADD. She did.

I started taking the same prescription drugs my younger brother used to take in grade school. The same ones I hadn't needed when my dorm-mates were pulling all-nighters with me at UC Berkeley and UCLA. *Concentration, concentration was the game,* except I was no longer good at it. Now, I not only had to take meds to help me focus, but also different pills for my anxiety; the stress of the job was undoing me—not that medication was entirely new to me. I had been on anti-depressants, first as a kid at my parents' behest (starting with Prozac at age ten), and then as a young adult of my own volition (Paxil and Wellbutrin made the rotations on multiple different occasions). Hashtag: family history of mental illness. But now, I had two choices. I could wait to be fired or quit. Being that decision-making is one of my worst traits, perhaps a symptom of the very thing I was now being medicated for—my attention deficit—I waited. In delaying the inevitable, I was proving both my "failure to make a decision" and "the decision to have failed" (Renee Gladman, "Five Things," the *Paris Review*). I straddled both with equal precision at a time when nothing else I did felt precise.

As soon as I was let go, and thus no longer reporting into work, I flushed all of the medication. I slept for a few days to combat more built-up exhaustion and then put my energies into seeking out continuing education to supplement my existing Pilates certification, as I simultaneously looked for full-time, paid Pilates opportunities. Even while attempting to balance the job from hell, I had been teaching both eighth grade English (for one hour a day) *and* Pilates part-time (on evenings and Saturdays)—no wonder my head was spinning. But now, even unmedicated, I could focus well-enough to lead my clients through a rigorous exercise regimen, although an errant phone buzzing in someone's purse or a kid playing noisily on his mom's iPad in the waiting room could still throw me off my game momentarily. Still, it was clear to me that my concentration was improving markedly. Better yet, I was no longer anxious.

A student of the Pilates method myself, I continued to hone this concentration muscle as I simultaneously toned my abdominals, glutes, hamstrings, triceps, inner and outer thighs, hips, and lats—all part of the core or trunk that we industry-folk refer to as the "Pilates Powerhouse," "center," and "box of the body." The beauty of classical Pilates—Pilates that is taught most closely to how its founder Joseph Pilates originally created it—is that there is an order to the exercises so that they flow from one to the next. Mr. Pilates famously said that his movement modality was the "complete coordination of mind and body." Mastering *complete coordination* takes extreme focus, and, more and more, I was starting to find it. Just as my body maneuvered itself into backbends and walk-overs, so too was my brain doing mental gymnastics, racing to always be one step ahead of my body in anticipation of what came next. As the months and years passed, and my communications manager role began to feel like a distant nightmare, I found I could train my mind—my interior—just as I was training my exterior, and I didn't need drugs to do it.

The full Reformer routine has over 50 exercises, and the mat has 34, both of which have a prescribed order. By 2019, I had built up the concentration necessary to remember each one, not only in my own body but also in my mind, so I could take an advanced client through them all when I was testing out of my continuing education "bridge" certification—a training program that builds on prior knowledge. But unlike learning the 50 states or the chronology of our US presidents—things I had done in school, which were relegated only to my short-term memory and then promptly forgotten—this information stuck. Pilates was forcing me to concentrate, despite my innate distractibility. Although I often felt I couldn't, I *had to* ignore the notifications popping up on my phone; the dust on the floor; the errant hair on my shirt; the wrinkles in my clothes; the conversations in the other room and really put my mind to the task at hand, lest I hurt myself or my clients. The practice was and remains: focus or fall.

Back in 2016, the systems I'd created—the Post-its, the pace, and even the planner my bosses had recommended—weren't working. But the Pilates system is always there for me: I fully support it, and it supports me in turn with the backing of a physical surface—be it a chair, mat, trapeze table ("the Cadillac"), or Reformer bed—and with the emotional support inherent in a mind-body movement practice. Even though, ten years in, I still often feel like a beginner because of the ways in which Pilates continuously humbles me, I am getting markedly better, stronger, and more focused by the day; and I get to pay that commitment forward to my students—many of whom may be struggling with attention issues themselves. I feel blessed, and am grateful to this ingenious method daily, for making me a viable player again in the concentration game of life.

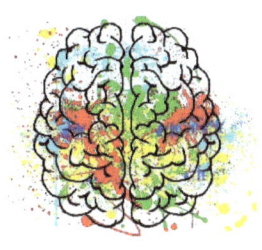

LOSING MYSELF

CANDACE MEREDITH

It wasn't long after he left that I lost touch with reality. I found myself adrift in a daze most days. Sometimes there was an interruption in losing myself when I would check the weather. The climate pulled me from a funk: a high of 30 degrees with wind chills to reach 60 miles an hour. With the wind whipping my face I became calmer. I could say his name and not shudder (shuddering from the wind was more amiable than loss and more conducive to having a good day). When I lost him I went into reverie of the first day we met; I dropped a bag of groceries leaving the market and he went down for the kill; picking up my bag of leaking milk he looked me in the eyes and said *here, I can help you with those.* I was hooked. He could have kept going but instead he helped lug the rest to the car. He told me his name was Richard. Richard and I dated for a year. Then he left. He left to hike the Appalachia via the Appalachian Trail and he wanted to do it alone. He had something to prove. He said he would be writing – to put his great adventure into a book – I wanted to be his story but instead I became the pages he would tear, would rip from the seams. Richard may be my past. But loving myself would be my future.

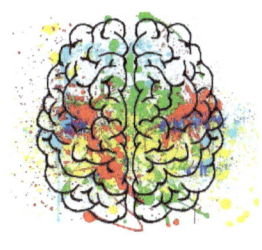

MORPHED INTO ME
CANDACE MEREDITH

I morphed there in front of him; my skin first turned to a wax so that my former self would be unrecognizable. He always said I needed to stop talking so my lips became more prominent – rounder, fuller, and red. In the sunlight my eyes turned to a gray unlike the hazel color they were and the wax looked cleaner like the shine to a bronze. My cheeks were raised, and my nose became slightly sharper. I didn't take the form of a doll in my real life – but a complicated human full of thoughts and ideas; this time I could speak of them even to nobody who was listening. I kept my plain-Jane name – it was, it is, Sarah. I am happy even as a ghost – a waxy one who has a full mouth and prominent cheek bones.

That is when I began to shine; the oppression left me bitter. It's a shame to say that he got the best of me. I wanted to be the mermaid in someone else's drama but in my own book I make all the rules – I morphed into the pages to become the thing I thought about most – a human morphed from clay; as the sculptor created my body I watched in awe because the curves were so unique. That is when I began to see myself a little better – in a painter's eye. The artist was Bill or Ted, someone lacking an identity because in this scenario names are not necessary. His hands developed my breasts to be painted by the others and in the figure I had a rump his hands wanted to touch. Bill took the gray out of my eyes with the stroke of his hand and then he was ready for the paint.

I resisted the urge to tell him You are My Creator! But I stayed in my place as he morphed my skin into a plastic sheathe and I became like a doll or a figure they gloated over – the art students who paint what the teacher sculpts. I was the model who still could not speak but from the wax-like doll I could utter a symphony with those lips, and I could taste the fun of becoming a me again, like a re-birth, like a woman who could breathe beyond the wax – in the hands of another man. I am Sarah! I said with eyes as deep as the soul – deep as the red on my lips, as vivid as the bronze of my skin, and the curves contoured beneath that mini skirt. When he created the new me I became more alive, like a gust of wind that moved my hair; she was me – a figure made of clay, painted like wax, and as I became sculpted then painted, I was re-born not just into a being but into a voice – and I could sing too, finally, because an artist shone me as everything I could be; what I already was…

Unlike he never did.

So, goodbye.

Love,

Sarah

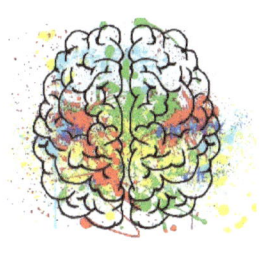

UNTITLED

CANDACE MEREDITH

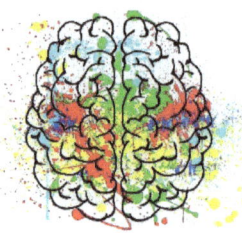

UNTITLED

CANDACE MEREDITH

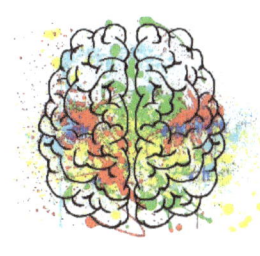

UNTITLED

CANDACE MEREDITH

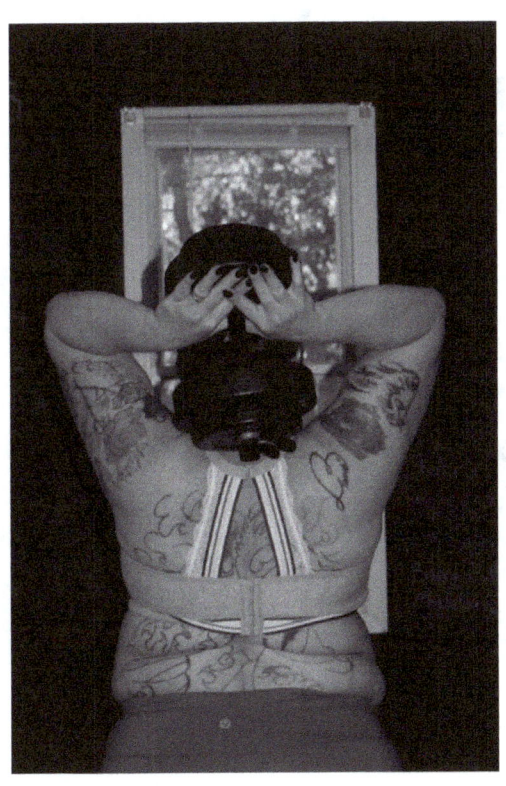

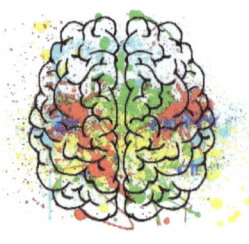

UNTITLED

CANDACE MEREDITH

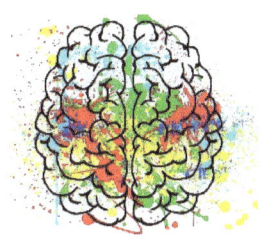

UNTITLED

CANDACE MEREDITH

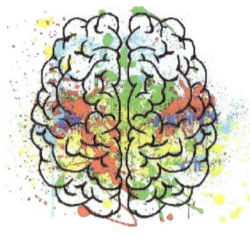

PLACID LAKE

MARTINE CRITCHLOW

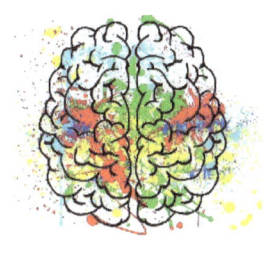

SUNBEAM ON WATER

MARTINE CRITCHLOW

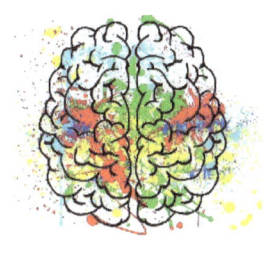

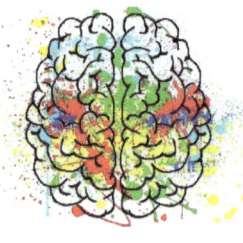

PEACEFUL GULLS
MARTINE CRITCHLOW

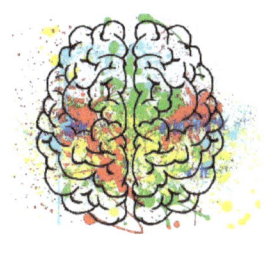

RED SETTING

MARTINE CRITCHLOW

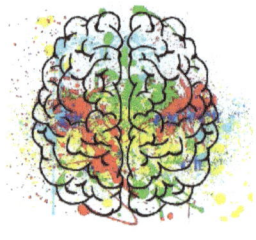

BRANCHES

MARTINE CRITCHLOW

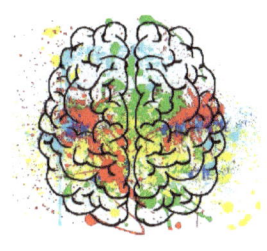

FOREST

SYDNIE BEAUPRÉ

This forest has teeth,

they snap, they gnash,

they cause my heart to

s-stutter in fear.

The trees have limbs,

roots that trip me at every

opportunity, the branches that

grab

at my vulnerable body.

Fear spikes through my veins,

and it tastes vicious, burning

the back of my throat.

Feet pounding, I run towards

the unknown,

and the idea scares me more than

staying here, in this forest of teeth and

limbs.

But then the trees part,

the clouds clear,

and I can finally see you.

You were with me this

whole time. You are my moon.

I point my snout to the

stars and sing my love for you,

I love you,

I love you,

I love you.

And I know you love me too by the silent

way you bathe me in your light, by the

way that you never leave my side

even when I can't

see you.

The forest may have teeth and limbs,

but I do, and you give me the

strength to

use them.

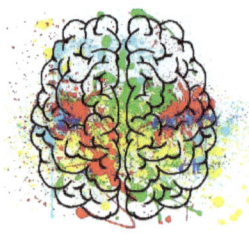

TRUE NORTH
SYDNIE BEAUPRÉ

When I am lost and know

not where to turn, she

is there for me, my true

north, guiding me home

where I belong, safe and sound.

When the world is cold

and I need a place to hide,

she is there for me, my true

north, guiding me home

where I belong, safe and sound.

When it all feels like

too much, and my heart's

about to explode, she is there

for me, my true north, guiding

me where I belong, safe and sound.

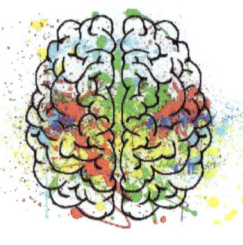

NO MERCY
SYDNIE BEAUPRÉ

I dance in the dark,

I've learned not to

fear the susurrus echoes

and haunting screams

that punch through the

night like a fierce kick

to the gut, and when the

monsters make an appearance

I laugh in their faces

for I alone hold the true power

and there will be no mercy

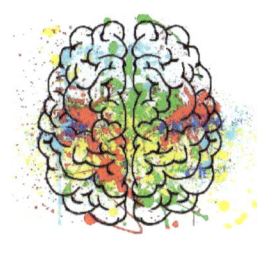

SUCCUMB

SYDNIE BEAUPRÉ

The scent of death hangs

high in the air, my

heart t-t-trembles

My veins explode, and

my energy leaves

my body, as I

succumb to the void.

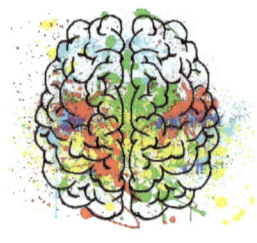

MY LOVE
SYDNIE BEAUPRÉ

His eyes are the

four leaf clovers

I always find, full

of secrets and

stories to be told.

His hands are the

sea, rough but

soothing, inviting

yet deadly, always

capable of keeping

me afloat.

His words are music,

lilting and steady, a

harmony meant only

for me.

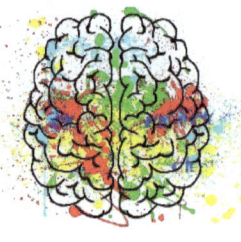

TEARS

SYDNIE BEAUPRÉ

Bottle my tears from my

Haunting mirrors, for they

Weep when they grow weary

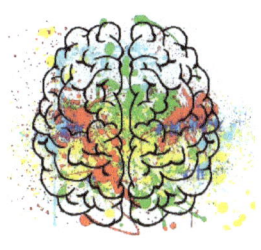

PROMISE

SYDNIE BEAUPRÉ

The sun is warming

our skin

cradling our bodies

in the heat that if

basked in for too

long could burn us whole.

But we don't care

we are

not quite broken yet

and we still believe in

the fairy tales of

our lost childhoods.

It was in those days

that we

learned that the sun

was going to explode one

day and leave the

earth completely engulfed.

Nobody knows when

it will

happen exactly when

the Earth will be one big

ball of flame and become the thing

we tried to protect ourselves from.

In this suspended apocalypse

it feels

as if we are the only two people

left who could possibly even

begin to know what it is like

to have nowhere left to go.

I remember when

my father

went outside and

said he'd be only a moment

but he lied and

he never came back.

I remember when

your mother

told you that she didn't love you

even though you were a son

and that was all

she had ever wanted.

If this world were

truly ending

I don't know that

anybody would know if

we were here and I think

that if nothing else, we have the Super-Nova-Promise of

The sun.

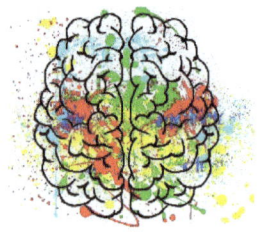

ONE

SYDNIE BEAUPRÉ

Whispers pressed against

my collar bones.

Our hearts in

their cages beating

in tandem. We're

gasping, breathless, creatures,

our pupils dilated,

and we are

one.

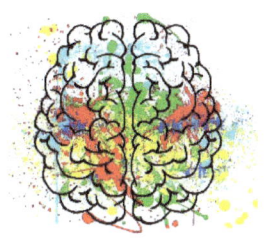

SOMETIMES
SYDNIE BEAUPRÉ

Sometimes I scream

in the dark of my mind

and sometimes I'm quiet,

seething with unbridled

rage at the atrocities of

this plagued world we

live in.

Sometimes I claw

At my confines, these walls

that surround my soul

and I weep, all snot, drool,

tears, and something intangible,

and I curse the names of those

who have done me wrong.

Sometimes I wonder

what it would be like to

be born into another body,

another century, another universe,

and so I put those thoughts down

for others to read, and I bare

my soul for all to see.

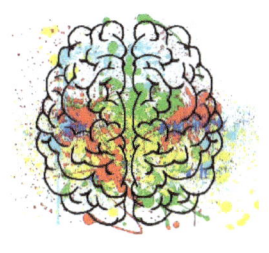

BEAUTY

SYDNIE BEAUPRÉ

In the Kingdom of Theluria, there was a village that was said to have been the oldest village in all of the land. It was so old, that it was said to have been the first village established in the whole Kingdom. It was a charming place, full of laughter and light, and beautiful old architecture and it was called Kathura.

Beside the village was a thick forest, through which there was a path. This path led to the most darling little cottage, that had sat abandoned and unkept for many years. Covering the house was all sorts of vegetation, but the most fascinating thing that covered the house, was the Roses.

It was covered in red, thorny, roses, among the vines.

The people of Kathura believed that an old witch had lived there prior to its abandonment, and they respected her, leaving offerings on the doorstep of the rose and vine covered cottage, offerings like meals and clothing and even money. They believed that her spirit kept Kathura safe from harm, and so, every harvest they gave her their offerings.

These offerings always mysteriously vanished the next day, leaving no trace of ever having been placed on the doorstep.

To the people of Kathura, this was their version of normal. It was something they didn't question.

That was, until a little girl of no more than six years old from a neighbouring village and her father happened to be passing through town. They were warned away by the village people, told that it was a sacred place only to be visited on the harvest and it was *not* the harvest.

But the father and child didn't listen. They wanted to see the pretty cottage, pick the pretty roses.

That was their mistake.

My name is Isabelle Havish, and when I was six, my father and I, homeless vagabonds at the time due to our previous home having been burnt down in a terrible fire, were passing through the village of Kathura, when we stopped by a pretty house. The townspeople told my father and I not to go there, not to touch the roses, but my father was foolish, and I was just a child, so I followed him down the path to the pretty house with all the roses, and I was *amazed*.

I had never seen so many roses.

My father hadn't either. He also hadn't seen such a beautiful, abandoned space before, he said aloud, in all his years on this earth. He couldn't believe that nobody was living here, that a house had just fallen into our laps. I was happy too, tired of wandering from town to town, looking for a permeant home. We'd been through three neighbouring towns in three years, and I hated not being able to settle down in one stable place.

I was a frustrated child. While he was busy trying to fight the vines to get to the front door, I decided to a simple thing. A very childish thing. Despite what the villages had said, a part of me felt rebellious and I decided to pick one of the roses for myself to keep, the villagers be damned. Instantly, I knew I'd made a terrible mistake when the flower started to wilt in my hands way too rapidly to be normal.

After my father braved the vines that had been blocking the front door, he was able to push it open, and we got our first peak at the inside of what would become our new home.

It was quaint, and elegant and it looked *occupied.*

"Hello?" Father called. "Is there anybody here?"

Nobody answered, so he took my hand and pulled me inside of the cottage, the rose still in my other hand, freshly picked.

"Haalloo!" Father bellowed.

It terrified the absolute wits out of us, when, before our eyes, an old woman appeared.

"How rude," she said. "Didn't you know not to come here until the harvest?"

Father blushed. "Well I thought it was an old folk tale, and thought this place abandoned. I'm terribly sorry for intruding. My daughter and I are homeless and seeking shelter."

"Shelter you will find here," the old woman said. "But it comes with a price. Your daughter killed one of my children, and for that I cannot forgive you."

He stepped back. "She did no such thing. You're mad."

"The rose," the old woman pointed at me. I was hiding behind my father's legs. "Your daughter picked one of my roses. My plants are my babies: I feel their pain. I felt the death of that rose deep in my soul."

My father tried to logic with her. "She's just a child! She didn't know any better."

"Ah, but the villagers warned you about the roses, did they not?"

"I am a man of Science!" my father shouted, "I am a man of logic. An inventor. You are not a witch nor the ghost of one, but a simple old crone."

The old woman came fast at me and took the now crushed and completely withered rose from her my hand. "It's okay my darling, your death will bring new life," she crooned to the flower. To my father, she said, "Your daughter is hereby *cursed*. Every harvest, the people of the village make sacrifices to my spirit. She has until eighteen to find true love, or on her eighteenth birthday she will turn forevermore into a terrible beast. Every harvest season she will become said beast for however long the season lasts."

"The harvest begins in October," my father whispered, horrified. "That means for most of October through to November, my daughter will become a beast?"

"Exactly, dear," said the old lady. "And she must never leave this village, or she will die."

My father, a man of Science, was floored.

"You're a real witch," he said, and she nodded. "Yes. And you will get to know me, as my new housemates."

"You mean, we can stay here, at least?"

"Of course. I will teach your daughter the arts while she stays here, and you can work on your inventions all you like while you live here. You will be provided for. But as I said, it comes with a price. You wanted a home, and now you have one; don't look a gift horse in the mouth," she said sassily. "Really, I could have killed you both for disrespecting my home in such a manner. You're lucky that I could use the company."

And that is how I came to live here, in this house. That is my curse. Every harvest, I become a wolf for however long the harvest lasts, and my eighteenth birthday is in a year.

I fear I will turn into a wolf for good, although when I am a wolf, life is simpler. Less complicated. I don't have to learn spells and potions and lotions and god knows what else Kathura has for me to study.

I simply run free in the woods and eat rabbits, keeping to myself, away from the village people for those few weeks a year.

The village people all know me as the strange but non-threatening girl who showed up one day with her father and took over the property. They don't know that I am cursed, but they know there's something *off* about me. And as for my father, they, as a small village run by religion, reject him during the day for being of the Scientific mind, and yet they constantly seek him out for his book knowledge – many of the villages occupants are illiterate and use him to do hard math and read any written word.

They're under the belief that I've always practiced the arts, that I came here a practitioner of magic, so they allow me to tend to their sick and wounded with the knowledge Kathura has imparted me with throughout these past years.

They allow me to play with their children, mingle with the other teens, but they keep it to a polite minimum.

That doesn't bother me, as I have learning to do, and Kathura is a strict teacher.

I've come to see her as sort of a grandmother figure in my life, despite the curse. She often says she wishes she could reverse it, but there is one thing she taught me; curses have no reversals.

I sigh, and close the window beside my bed, which I've been looking out of for at least fifteen minutes now, and roll over, frustratedly. I have work to do with the plants, and I don't feel like singing right now, however I've a feeling Kathura is going to pop into my room in a moment's notice if I don't get my behind outside, so I sit up, smooth out the creases of my dress, and make my way down the hall towards the stairs.

Kathura meets me there, smiling in that grandmotherly way she always does when she's with me. "Come now little one, it's time to sing to my babies."

She never grew out of calling me, *little one.*

But then again, she *is* technically ancient. She's who the whole village is named for! In her day, she was a powerful witch who helped secure peace for the Kingdom of Theluria. She came up against many other powerful witches from different Kingdoms, all sent to destroy what King Theluria was trying to build, and she came out victorious. She fought and won entire battles against hordes of soldiers, to secure the land that our village occupies, for the King of that time, and she built her own cottage with her bare hands and hard work.

That is how she came to be a near-deity to the villagers. Her use of the craft was astounding.

She was so strong, that when she died, her spirit materialized and she simply became a new being. A ghost that could still perform the arts from beyond the grave.

She can still drink, she can still eat; she just doesn't *have* to. She does it out of habit and because she enjoys it. It makes her feel more normal, being technically *dead*.

I follow her down the steps and through the foyer, and through the doorway full of vines. We make our way outside into what she calls her garden.

Vines and roses occupy the entire space, just as it was when I came here years ago.

Kathura pops off, leaving the work to me once she sees that I've bought my bell set, strapped to my hip by a bandolier.

Or my Belle set as she calls it. She's fond of puns.

I take out the smallest bell, Kin, and ring it once. I take out the second smallest, Ken, and ring it once, too. The last bell, the biggest, I ring twice. Its name is Kan.

I recite the words I learned by heart at age seven. "*Dathos a hanik*," I chant, "Dathos a hanik *mal*", before singing high and clear, "I manifest positive energy into this space, leaving only peace in chaos's place."

The plants around me soak up the positive magic happily. I can feel their energy, as Kathura has taught me to, as if it were my own. I push all of the positive magic into the flowers and vines, and they sparkle with life.

Dew even kisses the roses, as if a morning drizzle has just fallen upon their tender flesh.

My duty in the front done, I move behind the cottage, to where there are more roses and vines. I ring Kin, and then

Ken, and finally Kan, and then *"Dathos a hanik,"* I chant, "Dathos a hanik *mal*. I manifest positive energy into this space, leaving only peace in chaos's place."

I'm so into what I'm doing, that I don't notice him at first.

He's new.

Not from our village.

And he's staring at me like he's never seen anything more amazing in his life.

"The rumours are true then," the red-haired boy says, looking like one of the Roses from the garden. "You practice magic."

"Who's asking?" I'm defensive, and I don't know why. I don't like this boy being up in what's come to be known as *my* space.

"Colt. Colt Friar. It's nice to make your acquaintance, Ms..."

"Isabelle Havish. You can call me Belle. And you're trespassing on our property you know, which isn't polite," I say, still wary. "It's how my father and I got stuck here in the first place. Kathura won't welcome *another* trespasser."

He cocked his head. "So what the say is true? The old lady's ghost still haunts this place?"

"Maybe," I say. "Maybe not. Maybe it's *another* Kathura."

"Well it's not a very popular name these days," he says, grinning. "Ms. Magic maker."

"You don't need to call me that just because I practice the arts," I'm blushing. "Anyone could do it with the right training, really."

"Is that so?" he sounds genuinely curious. "Well, I'm new around here, and have never seen the arts up close, so it's an honour to have made your acquaintance in such a magical place."

My father picks just that moment to walk out of the back door, and right then, I wish I knew how to curse people properly because he deserves to be cursed for interrupting the only *new* person I'd come across in years.

One who thins I'm *interesting*.

People don't really pass through our town since my father and I took up residence. It's now known as a village full of mystery, with the whole is Kathura dead or isn't she question. And the whole sacrificing to her on the harvest thing seems to have put off new visitors from coming since we arrived, since they've started to leave sacrifices for *us*.

As I said, the village people interact with me, but they keep their distance unless they need something from me; the kids make exceptions because they're too young to have biases against me because of what I am. I make my rounds daily to tend to the sick or old, and I've cured many ailments that wouldn't have been able to be cured if not for the arts, but I do wish the people would treat me as a human girl and not a miracle worker who should be revered and feared, slightly.

"What's this?" Father asks. "A newcomer? How pleasant! Oh we haven't had any visitors since the last outbreak of the consumption. What do you need from us, son?"

"I don't need anything," Colt says, awkwardly. "I just came to check out whether the rumours about this place were true or not, and they seem to be…well, sort of true. And that's kind of amazing," he continues. "I'll get out of your hair."

"No," Pops in Kathura, absolutely terrifying Colt, sending him nearly ten feet in the air. "You won't be leaving, my sweet boy, you'll be remaining here."

"Oh my Gods," he says, blinking and rubbing his eyes. "I'm seeing the spirit of The Kathura. I think I'm about to lose consciousness."

Kathura glide/walks towards him, and he backs up in fear. "D-don't hurt me."

I laugh. "Kathura? Hurt you? She might *curse you* for trespassing, but she wouldn't *hurt* a fly."

Colt shakes his head. "That's not what I heard. This is not what I'm seeing. I'm in a dream."

Kathura pops out of our plane for a second, and bursts right back into our plane, right in Colt's face. "And cursed he will be. Now, what's a good curse for simple trespassing and talking to my charge. Let me think. Hmm, a stationary curse. You're a boy that likes to travel, that plans to make it to the University that Mr. Havish here taught at years ago. You're an orphan and are penniless. You were hoping to get work in this town when you arrived, but the townspeople made you curious about the girl and her father who live in the forbidden cottage. I can see your past and your future, and your present is this: you may not leave this property for a year's worth of time, and you must help my apprentice. You will become *her* apprentice."

"No!" I shout, "That's not fair! You can't just *do* that, Kathura. He has work he has to go back to."

She smiles, sagely. "I just did."

I show Colt to his new quarters, which is the room next to mine. My father sleeps in his workshop usually, which is an outbuilding a bit farther into the woods than the cottage but his room is across from mine. His workshop is high up in-between two big oak trees, where nobody can bother him. He built it himself, with a bit of help from Kathura – she gave him the gold to afford the materials he needed to build it, since a dead woman can't use gold.

The villagers never questioned it, and just accepted that he was using their sacrificial gold to pay them back what they'd given in the first place.

Colt stands awkwardly at his door, his bag of worldly possessions having been on his person when he was cursed, thank Gods, unsure of what to do. "So, this is all real, and I'm not going to wake up?" he asks.

I nod. "Yeah. Your ass is *cursed*."

"I can't believe I get to stay here for a year, though," he says, his voice full of awe. "I'm an orphan with nothing, as your witchy friend mentioned earlier, and I literally came here with everything I owned on me. The Inn I'm staying at will probably just assume I've up and left them, which is a shame as they were rather nice owners."

"Oh Kathura won't want you to stay hidden, and she'll give you money to pay off your debts. She'll want you on display to the town as her new play-thing. She's like a big kid."

"Oh, is she…" he muses, sounding nervous. "What will she want me to do as your apprentice."

I invite him into my room, and he sits right down on my bed which makes me blush as I've never had a man in my room before, not counting Father. And now that I look at Colt, I can see that he is more man than boy. He must be at least two years older than me, and he's not weak bodied in appearance. In fact, he looks as strong as Father, which makes me blush even more because that's pretty strong for someone his age.

He's got that look to him like he could win a fight against five men through both logic and his fists.

He's the first man to ever make me feel…like a *woman*.

And I don't know how to feel about that.

"Oh, a number of things. You'll have to learn the names of the Bells first, and then the chant for the garden," I tell him, remembering my own early lessons.

"Is that so?" he asks, mystified.

"Mmhmm. And then, I'll have to teach you basic herb knowledge for the sick and elderly, so you can learn how to treat the easiest cases."

"Like what?" he runs a hand through his hair.

"You know, a cough, earache, that sort of thing. And then you'll move on to the tougher things, like illness of the mind and heart."

"How long will that all take?"

I shrug. "If you're a fast learner, no time at all. There's a lot of Science to the arts. I think you'll like it, if you were planning on going to the University my Father taught at. It's all about Science and Philosophy and Humanities. A lot of what I do falls under those categories."

He shrugs back. "I didn't know what I was going to take there anyway. I just knew I wanted to study something. Anything. I was tired of being an uneducated orphan."

"My mother died when I was born," I tell him. "I can't *imagine* losing Father. How long have you been an orphan?"

He scrubs a hand down his face. "My whole life. You can't imagine the hard work I've had to do is. Learning something new, something exciting? It's what I wanted to go to University for. To rise up and become something. To stop doing hard labour and start discovering a whole new world."

I laugh a little at that. "Well you've certainly fallen into a new world."

I don't tell Colt about my own curse right now because it feels like the wrong moment. What's the right moment to say, "Hey, I'm cursed too! And by the way, towards the end of *every* October I become a wolf for a *solid* amount of weeks. I have a year before I turn into a wolf *for good* because nobody from this village will get to know me as a person, let alone ever love me! Isn't that remarkable?"

No. Can't do that, now can I?

"I guess I have," he remarks, looking around my room, examining it. I've filled it all with things I love, so I'm slightly self-conscious as to what he thinks. I have dolls and stuffed animals, all given to me by Kathura, which is slightly embarrassing, but I also have my rock collection and my potion sets. I have books everywhere, books on whatever subject I can get my hands on.

He seems to like what he sees because he smiles. "I think I'm going to like living here."

It was May when Colt came to us, inexperienced and amazed by every magical thing he saw. Now, three months later, he's learned all of the names of the Bells, the chant, and the song.

When he sings it, it's deep and mournful, not at all like how I sing it. Sometimes we duet, chanting and singing together. Kathura likes it the best that way when we sing together. The plants seem to like it too.

It is the beginning of September, and I've grown unexpectedly close to Colt.

So close, that Kathura and my father have both noticed, and have become obsessed with the idea of him breaking my curse.

I told them that Colt could never love someone like me. A girl who turns into a beast.

No matter how close we've grown.

No matter how he makes me feel on the inside.

He's smart, and funny, and he has a thirst for knowledge that I find refreshing. I never knew that I loved to teach until I began to teach him. It awakened in me the *drive* share my knowledge, the motivation to do my daily duties with somebody other than myself – since Kathura has been trusting me since I was ten to do them myself.

Of course, I've only been doing my work in the village since I turned twelve, so I was holed up in the cottage learning the arts for nearly six years. That was when she came up with the idea that I should earn my place in the village. Until then the people had just sort of tolerated me as a charming little girl who had unfortunate parentage. They treated me at best, like an outsider. But when I started healing people, they realized I wasn't a threat, and started to trust me more, and more. Then they started to trust my father, at least a little bit.

So I was surprised that the religious villagers took so well to the new addition of Colt, because he was so *into* the arts and sciences, and they were so afraid of them.

I mean, they accepted me because I was young when I came to them, vulnerable. But Colt is nineteen, a man. An unknown man, who knows too many unknown things.

But the villagers love Colt.

The children *adore* playing with him, and the adults seem to trust him with them. The adults seem more open to him, than they were with myself and my father.

It makes me sort of proud to know that it's because we've reinforced ourselves as a part of this community whether they wanted us to or not. We've taken care of their ill, explained to the people tough questions that they wouldn't have known the answers to otherwise, helped them re-strengthen roofs.

We've connected these laypeople to the use of electricity, the wonders of the written word and to science, although they have a long way to go. They never would have accepted Colt had it not been for my father and I helping them out.

And for his part, Colt has been nothing but happy to help the villagers when they come asking for it.

I can see myself falling for him, and it hurts deeply, because I know in nearly eight months I'll be a wolf and *he'll* be free to go to the University, like he'd originally planned. We'll have to part ways.

And isn't parting such sweet sorrow?

October comes fast, and I know it's time I have to explain to Colt the nature of my own curse. He's asked time and again how my father and I came to live in this village, and we've always circled around the answer, like it'll soften the blow.

But now? Kathura says it's time to try. Not to give up, and willingly let the curse take me. And she's the one who placed the curse on me in the first place!

It's after our shift at the village hospital, that I tell him.

It's cold, and the sweater I'm wearing isn't enough to keep me warm, and Colt's just given me his, but I bite out the words even though they're bitter on my tongue.

"I have a story for you, Colt. One that's especially important. It's mine and my father's."

"Tell me," he says gently. "You know I've always been curious."

"Alright," I whisper. "I'll tell you everything when we get home, and after we've rung the Bells. But you have to promise not to think of me any differently afterwards."

He seems conflicted but promises. "How could I think anything bad about you when all you've ever been is kind to me? When all you've ever done is teach me things I never knew I wanted to learn? When you've given me a home, and food, and clothes?"

"You'll probably change your opinion of me when you find out my secret."

"I won't," he says earnestly, and a part of me wants to believe him.

When we make it home, we do our duties diligently, and after dinner, the two of us retire to the back garden. I sit down on one of my favourite stone benches, and Colt sits next to me.

"In the Kingdom of Theluria," I start, "there was a village that was said to have been the oldest village in all of the land. It was so old, that it was said to have been the first village established in the whole Kingdom. It was a charming place, full of laughter and light, and beautiful old architecture and it was called Kathura. Beside the village was a thick forest, through which there was a path. This path led to the most darling little cottage, that had sat abandoned and unkept for many years. Covering the house was all sorts of vegetation, but the most fascinating thing that covered the house, was the roses. It was covered in red, thorny, roses, among the vines."

"I think I know the place," he says, captivated by the story already.

"The people of Kathura believed that an old witch had lived in the cottage prior to its abandonment and they respected her spirit, leaving offerings on the doorstep of the rose and vine covered cottage, offerings like meals and clothing and even gold. They believed that her spirit kept Kathura safe from harm, and so, every harvest they gave her their offerings, and they remained safe. These offerings always mysteriously vanished the next day, leaving no trace of ever having been placed on the doorstep."

This he knows already, but still, he listens when I speak, always respectful.

"To the people of Kathura, this was their version of normal. It was something they didn't question."

He nods, and motions for me to go on. "That was, until a little girl of no more than six years old from a neighbouring village and her father happened to be passing through town. They were warned away by the village people, told that it was a sacred place only to be visited on the harvest and it was *not* the harvest. But the father and child didn't listen. They wanted to see the magical abandoned cottage with the roses and the vines. That was their first mistake."

He keeps listening for more. "So, what was their second mistake?"

"The girl picked one of the flowers," Kathura pops in and says in my place, looking sad. "And so in anger, I cursed her. I believed her act to be beastly, and so I cursed her to become one."

Colt looks confused now. "What do you mean? A beast? There's nothing *beastly* about Belle. She's..." he blushes, "Stunning."

I look down. "During the harvest, I turn into a beast for weeks at a time. I live in the woods, by the village. I hunt small game, and *never* hurt people."

He looks between Kathura and I, and at first looks as if there's something funny, and then his expression changes, as his belief in my story rises. Then he looks at me as if he's never seen me before. "You become *a beast?*"

I nod. "Yes. And I will continue to do so until I turn eighteen. Then, I'll remain a beast until I die."

His eyes widen. "You can't break the curse?"

I shake my head. "You know as well as I do that that's impossible to do."

I long to tell him about the clause, but knowing he'll be free in seven months to pursue his dreams makes me not want to tell him the part about true love. About how I feel for him.

"What kind of beast," Colt questions, surprising me. "What kind of beast do you turn into. I need to know so I can picture it."

I didn't expect him to care. "A wolf," I admit. "I turn into a wolf."

He thinks this over carefully, giving nothing away.

I'm sure that this is it.

He's going to reject me.

Instead, he says, "So how much time left do we have left?"

"Her day of birth is in March," Kathura answers for me. "She has five months before she turns into a wolf forever."

"And there is no way to break the curse?" he asks, sounding desperate. "I just started to get to know you. I wanted to spend *years* studying under you, even after my curse is up. I like living here with you and Mr. Havish and even with you, Kathura. I don't even want to go to the University anymore, now that I live here."

"There *is* one way," Kathura says, and I beg her with my eyes not to tell him, but she does, ever defiant, and I begin to cry uncontrollably when she says, "I cursed Isabelle to turn into a wolf forevermore on her eighteenth birthday, unless she found her one true love."

"Why are you crying?" Colt asks. Comming over to me, and brushing my tears away with his thumbs, holding my face in his hands. So gently…. "Didn't you know? *I* am in love with you Belle, you idiot. Your curse has already been broken."

I'm crying so much that I'm shaking. "What do you mean?"

"You won't turn into a wolf this month," Kathura says, "or any other day of the year, anymore my darling girl."

Father, always bad at timing, opens the door and interprets the situation completely wrong.

"Why is my baby crying?" he asks, "Colt, what did you do?"

"He did it, Father," I cry, happily. "He broke my curse."

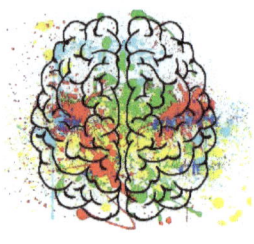

VICTORIOUS

SYDNIE BEAUPRÉ

My name is Victoria Honda. I am not a normal seventeen-year-old girl. I've been training with warriors since I was five years old. They are warriors who fight evil spirits known to us as yokai. My father is their – our – sensei. We are called Essence warriors, as we manipulate the essence of these evil yokai using our own magic.

My father teaches that not all yokai are evil, but that we shouldn't get into a yokai's business unless we're prepared to take on a great burden.

I for one can't see myself ever taking on that great a burden. I train with the warriors, but I don't fight with them. I'm only seventeen, after all. Getting into a yokai's business is a burden I do not wish to undertake.

Right now I'm at school in homeroom, and I'm talking to the new boy named Hunter. He's tall and slender, with red hair and amber eyes. He's got a scar running the length of his right eyebrow. He's popular already because he's nice, but he's only been here for two days. He hasn't made any close friendships yet.

"So you've got a parent from Japan, too?" I ask, and he nods.

"Yeah," he says. "How did you know?"

"I could just tell," I say honestly. "Your cheekbone structure and your last name."

He blushes. "I guess it's easy with a last name like Saito."

"Yeah, well mine is Honda, so I think I know how you feel."

"Painfully non-white at a mostly white high school?" Hunter asks.

I laugh. "Yes, pretty non-white."

"So, you want to get to know more about me, huh?" he asks.

I nod. "So what if I do. You're likable and we share the whole Japanese thing."

"Do you like anime?'

"Yeah, I love it."

"You pass my test," he says. "I think I like you, Honda."

"Please, call me Victoria."

"Victoria then," he says.

More people file into the room, and I walk away, thinking that it would be cool to have a friend who is just like me.

###

"We are going to learn about countering a bakemono," my father says to the class. "It's a simple magical move. Who can tell me how it's done?"

Nobody but me raises their hand.

"Anybody besides Victoria."

Nobody raises their hand.

"Fine," my father says. "I'll tell you how. You reflect their current form back at them and it confuses them, dropping their glamour."

Neal, a man who is all hard angles and sharp glances, says, "Damn it, I knew after all."

My father turns on him, annoyed. "You should have said something, Neal."

"It's because he's scared of being wrong," I announce, and my father turns on me.

"Victoria! We do not need that attitude of yours. You can leave for today. Come back when class is finished to help everybody pack the mats up."

I sigh, but comply, walking out into the crisp evening air. I walk the streets of Montreal, careful not to go too far. A movement down an alley catches my eye and I follow it, my yokai senses tingling.

I'm not disappointed, because when I turn into the alley I come fave to face with a large fox yokai. But upon closer inspection, I realize that it's a glamour. I'm not seeing his true form.

"You're a yokai," I gasp, amazed.

The fox has been wounded on its shoulder, and I'm startled when it speaks to my mind.

I was shot by another spirit. He's the head of a gang of malevolent spirits. I tried to stop him from hurting a human and he shot me instead, he says

"Drop your glamour," I demand. "I can't help you if you're working to hold it. I need you in your true form to heal you."

I didn't ask you to heal me, he says, cautiously. I don't trust you.

"You're going to have to trust me," I tell him. "I can heal you. I'm an Essence Warrior."

Ah you're one of those who fight that bad spirits. In that case you can heal me, but I want to remain in this form.

There's no other choice then. I reflect his glamour back at him with a few words, and he quickly drops it in confusion.

"Hunter?" I ask, amazed at who is standing before me.

It's Hunter, but it's not. He has ears like a fox and a large bushy tail.

"Damn it Victoria!" he says, "Why'd you do that?"

"It was the only way I could get you to drop the glamour," I tell him. "Sorry, but if I'm going to heal you, I need you in your true form."

I walk over to him, and place my hands on his shoulder.

"Stitch together," I tell his wound, and it does.

"Ow that stings," Hunter says. "Shit."

"I'm sorry, Hunter. Never said it wouldn't hurt." I tell him.

When I'm done healing him, I take a step back, and look him over.

He looks like something out of an anime or manga. "So, you're a yokai," I tell him.

"Half," he says. "My mother is human."

"And she willingly mated with a yokai?" I ask, confused.

Hunter bristles. "Yes. She fell in love with his human glamour. By the time she found out he was a spirit, she was pregnant with me. He was killed by another spirit when I was five, and we moved to Canada after that, for a new life. She thought that the spirits here might be kinder than those in Japan."

"And?" I ask.

He sighs. His ears flatten against his head, and his tail flicks. "Most spirits don't accept halflings. They consider us bad luck."

"I'm sorry," I tell him. "I don't think you're bad luck."

"You haven't spent much time with me," he says. "But anyway, thanks for healing me Victoria. I should get going, or my mom is going to worry."

"I'll see you at school tomorrow?" I ask, hopefully.

He sighs and puts on his human glamour. "I'll see you tomorrow."

We both leave the alley, and head in opposite directions.

When I get back to the studio, it's just in time to help put away the mats. I dutifully help out, and when I'm done, I lean against one of the stacks of mats and wait for my father.

When he's finished talking to the class's stragglers, he makes his way toward me.

"So, what did you do with yourself while I slaved away teaching?" he asks.

I debate telling him the truth, but I remember what he always says about getting into the business of a yokai; not to do it unless I'm ready for a great undertaking.

"I met a friend from class," I tell him, bending the truth. "We hung out for a few minutes."

Dad smiles, and pats me on the back. "Good. You need to be more social outside of school."

I internally cringe. I'm social in school, sure, but I have no close friendships. It's something of a sore spot.

"Yeah, it was nice," I say. "I'll have to hang out with him again."

###

I get to class early. Only a few students are here, sitting at their desks dutifully studying or reading. I make my way to my desk, and sit. And then I wait.

Hunter gets to class ten minutes later, thankfully. I stand and walk up to him, as he gets to his own desk.

"Can we talk?" I ask.

He frowns. "I have a feeling I'm not going to like this talk."

I roll my eyes. "You'll survive it. I just want to ask you a few questions."

We head into the hallway, where nobody is milling around, luckily.

"What is it," he asks, nervous.

"Who shot you," I ask. "I train to fight evil yokai, so it's my job to stop them from committing crimes like that, or it will be when I'm done my training. You said he was going to shoot a human and shot you instead. What happened last night, Hunter?"

He sighs, and I imagine his tail flicking and his ears flattening. "Their names are Henri Forcette, Jessie Gunner and Will Yates. They go to this school, so I'm sure you know their names."

He's right, I do know their names. They're trouble makers that are constantly getting into fights and stealing from other students.

"Which one shot you?"

"Henri. I stumbled on them in an alley, they had their gun pointed at some poor human. They were trying to rob him, I think. But I told them to leave, and the human got away. Then Jessie and Will grabbed me, and Henri kicked me in the gut. He said halflings should stay out of the business of spirits. That he needed to teach me a message."

"Where on earth would he even get a gun?" I ask, horrified. "He's seventeen."

"And he's not human," Hunter reminds me. "We can get our hands on things that normal people would have trouble attaining."

"They need to be stopped," I tell him. "I want to stop them."

He laughs. "You're just a girl," he says. "Sure you're an Essence Warrior in training, but what could you possibly do to stop them."

I bristle. "I've been training since I was five. I'm a prodigy."

"And you're still just one girl," he says gently. "I don't want you to put yourself in needless danger because of me."

I'm pissed off. "if I want to put myself into a dangerous situation Hunter, I will. I'm not going to do it right away, because I need time to prepare, time to train. But I will be the one who stops them, if somebody else doesn't get to them first."

Hunter looks upon me with a newfound look of respect. "Okay," he says. "You'll be the one who stops them. Do you know what that means?"

I nod. I might have to kill them.

"Do you think you can do it?"

"Absolutely."

###

After that day, Hunter and I began to hang out between my training sessions and school. We watch anime together, we talk about which manga or young adult book we're currently reading. We talk about everything and sometimes, we're silent, each on our phone or laptop, doing our own thing.

It's great to finally have a friend, even if he is half yokai.

He keeps his human glamour on even around his mother, which I find odd. You'd think that he'd be more comfortable in his true form at home. I've never asked him about it, though. It feels wrong.

Today, we're at his house, in his room watching a movie called A Silent Voice. It's a movie about a bully that becomes friends with the deaf girl he used to tease in elementary school. We're in the middle of the movie when I feel his eyes on me.

My eyes drift towards him, and he's looking at me.

Just looking.

My heart skips a beat.

"What?" I ask, feeling self-conscious.

And his smile is so big it could light up the room like the sun. "Nothing," he says.

I smile back. "That's not true."

His cheeks are turning red, "Okay, maybe I was thinking that you looked beautiful in this lighting. And some other things, too."

Oh my God. My heart. "You weren't," I say. "But if you were, what were those other things?"

His cheeks are a brilliant scarlet now. "I was thinking that I wanted to kiss you."

My own cheeks must be red too, but I say, "So then do it."

And he does.

My world explodes, the sun sets and rises and sets again behind my eyelids as we kiss.

When I open my eyes, I'm shocked.

Hunter has dropped his glamour.

"Oh, sorry," he says. "I didn't mean to."

I reach out and gently touch him behind the ear, petting him. "No, I like you the way you are. You don't have to look human for me."

He leans into my hand. "My own mother prefers it when I look human. Do you really not mind?"

I smile at him. "You're beautiful," I tell him honestly. "You have to know that."

He frowns. "Other spirits think I look too human. Most humans would think I'm a terrifying."

I lean in and kiss him on the nose. "I like you just how you are, Hunter."

This coaxes a smile out of him. "I think," he says. "I think I might be falling in love with you."

I lean in, and we kiss again. This time is even better than the first. "I think I might be falling in love with you," I tell him.

###

When my father meets Hunter for the first time, he's shocked. He can see through Hunter's glamour right away.

"A yokai?" he whispers at us. Louder, he says, "Do you know what I do, boy?"

Hunter nods. "You're an Essence Warrior, sir. You use magic to fight evil spirits. You call them yokai."

My father looks him over. "Yes," he says. "That's right. So you know that if you hurt my daughter I will come for you?"

Hunter actually answers like he's speaking to a drill sergeant. "Yes sir!"

My father smiles. "Ah well, as long as you know, welcome to my studio."

He is surprisingly more tolerant than I thought. Then again, he knows nothing of Henri and his gang and I plan to keep it that way.

And so Hunter begins to sit in on my lessons.

We grow closer, and closer, until three months have passed in the blink of an eye. We're officially on summer break.

"So, you've been training really hard recently," Hunter is saying to me. We're hanging out in his room and it's getting late.

"Yeah," I say, "I told you. I'm training to kick Henri and company's butts."

he frowns. "So you're still going to fight them."

"If that's what it takes to stop them, I'll do it. Have you heard the latest news? They robbed Yasmin Lachance recently and the authorities won't do anything about it."

He nods. "Yeah. I heard it was by gunpoint."

"I can't believe nobody has done something about them yet."

"Their glamours are good," Hunter says. "I'll give them that."

I nod, thoughtfully. "Yeah, they look hella human."

He laughs. "And I don't? I thought my glamour was pretty good."

I shake my head. "It's not that great. You still look slightly off, if somebody looks at you hard enough that is."

His tail is flicking from side to side, good-naturedly. "Okay, I kind of suck at my glamour. I admit defeat."

"So, I win," I say. "What do I win?"

He leans in and captures me with a kiss. "This," he says between kisses.

Eventually the kisses deepen. My shirt comes off.

"Oh my God," Hunter says. "You're beautiful."

I blush, and it travels all over my body. "No you. You're amazing," I tell him, and I mean it.

He looks like some sort of feral God.

His shirt follows mine soon after. And then our pants. And then, slowly, he asks, "You know I'm not fully human," he says, "But it all works the same. Anatomically, I mean. I just have big ears and a tail.

"I've guessed that much," I tell him honestly.

"And that really doesn't repulse you?" Hunter sounds so vulnerable that I dispel his worries with a kiss. "I love you."

And you can guess what happens next. I don't need to get into the details.

But, after, when he's on the edge of sleep in my arms, I sigh a sign of pure content. "I promise I won't get hurt when I go after Henri and company. I'm planning on doing it tomorrow."

He shifts, sleepily. "You can't promise that. Instead promise to try not to get hurt."

I chuckle. "I will try my best not to get hurt. And if I do get hurt, I can always heal myself."

"Mmph, that makes me feel a bit better," Hunter admits, nuzzling into my neck and purring.

I reach out and give him a scratch behind the ear. "Good," I say. "I don't want you to worry about me."

"I will anyway, you know," he says. "But I know how strong you are. I just love you and don't want you getting hurt."

"Well I love you too," I tell him. "And please, know that I've got this."

"It's your first battle," he says. "I hope you go into it fiercely."

I grin. "I will. I'll kick their asses."

###

Tonight is the night that I go looking for Henri. I got a tip from Julia Tabage that he likes to hang out near Atwater, so I hop on the metro from Saint-Laurent and make my way there.

It's close to the end of cufew and I know that I'm going to probably have to uber home after this. When I get to Atwater, I walk out of the mall and out onto the streets and start walking. Eventually I come to an alley, and, just like Julia said, There is Henri, Will and Jessie.

They're terrorizing a poor young yokai. She looks maybe twelve at most.

"Halflings are disgusting," taunts Will.

"You should be put down," Henri says, pointing his gun at her.

"Stop!" I shout and they all look at me. It gives the girl a chance to run, and she quickly hides behind me.

"Thank you," she says. "You're one of those magic humans, right? The ones who fight evil spirits?"

I nod. "Yes," I say to her. To Henri and his gang, I say, "I'm your worst nightmare."

Henri laughs. "You're from my school right? The girl who has the hots for that other halfling. The one I taught a lesson to?"

"His name is Hunter," I grit out. "You insufferable ass."

He cocks his gun, and points it at me. "Not so brave now are you, princess?"

I laugh. "You think that can stop me? Just watch me."

I snap my fingers and say, "Freeze." Everything around me freezes but me. I do a little skip towards Henri and pluck the gun right out of his ugly hands. Then, I punch him in the nose.

"Unfreeze," I say, and everything goes back to normal speed.

"What the fuck?" Henri shouts, cupping his broken nose. "How did you do that?"

I smile, sadistically. "I told you, I'm your worst nightmare. By the time I'm done with you, you won't harm another human or yokai – I mean spirit – ever again."

He steps back, in horror. "What the fuck?"

Will and Jessie however, believe that they can harm me. They've begun to walk in my direction. I laugh and say, "Freeze." Everything freezes again.

I kick Will in the stomach and knee Jessie in the groin. And then I bind them all with a spell. "You will do no more harm to human or spirit kind ever again. If you do, I will come for you and I will kill you. Make it so. Unfreeze."

Both boys double over in pain and I say, "I win."

I toss Henri the gun and compel him, "Get rid of this," I say. "And go home."

Henri simply begins to walk away, holding his broken nose in one hand.

"What did you do to him?" asks Jessie.

"What I'll do to you if you don't leave us, now."

They get the message and instantly leave me and the girl alone in the alley.

I turn to her. "What's your name?"

She beams at me. "Hannah Jaques."

"Well Hannah, it's nice to meet you. I'm Victoria," I tell her. "What school do you go to?"

"Lindsay Place," she says. "I know it's far but it's where my mom went."

"I smile. "My mom went there too."

She's still beaming. "Thank you for saving me Victoria."

"Somebody had to do something about those assholes."

Hannah nods. "They really are asshooles. I can't believe you went to school with them! What are the odds."

"I went searching for them today," I admit. "I was glad when I came across someone to save. I've been training for this day for a long time. I didn't even have to fight with them. I just used my magic."

"Well it was amazing," Hannah says. And then she gasps and says, "You don't think I'm evil do you?"

I laugh. "No, I don't think you're evil. In fact, my boyfriend is a halfling fox spirit."

"Wow, that's so cool. It's just like my mom and dad. My dad is a crow spirit."

I smile. "That's nice to know."

"Yeah," she says. "So, I have to get going, but if you want to keep in touch you can add me on Facebook or Instagram."

And I find that I do genuinely want to keep in touch.

###

When I get to Hunter's he's at the door like a puppy, tail wagging and ears flat.

"Are you hurt?"

I laugh. "It was so easy that it was boring."

He blinks at me. "No way."

I nod. "Yes way. They won't be hurting anybody again, and if they do, my spell will alert me and I will kill them if I have to."

"And that's it. We get to live happily ever after?"

I laugh. "Yes," I say. "They won't ever bother anybody again. We can live life in relative safety. There will always be other yokai who are a threat, but not to you and I. We get our happily ever after."

I lean in to kiss him and he meets me halfway. "Why don't you come on in," he says, "and tell me exactly how it all went down."

So, I do.

And so that's the end of that.

My name is Victoria Honda, and I am an Essence Warrior. I am in love with a half-yokai. I am not a normal seventeen-year-old. And I wouldn't have it any other way.

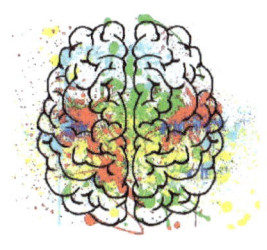

SUCH UNSTABLE ENERY
SYDNIE BEAUPRÉ

My friends Darren and Josh left hours ago, and it's nearing the end of the event. I'm high as hell on molly and speed, and I've had a few beers; I'm fucked up. Plus, I've fed from the Energy around me, so I'm nice and full for once.

I'd been starving myself again, until today, denying myself any Energy.

I don't want to be here anymore now that I'm full.

I need my best friend Spencer – my other half – but I don't have a cellphone anymore. My dad smashed it in a fit of rage because I stole a pack of his smokes a few weeks ago. I need a pay phone.

Where am I again?

Think.

Lionel Groulx?

No.

Think, Cayden. Block out the voices and the people around you. Block out the music.

Saint-Laurent...?

I ask some rando, who confirms my guess. I'm near Saint Laurent metro.

I leave the event and walk until I get to the payphone I need, digging change out of my pocket.

"Hello?" She picks up on the third ring. "Cayden?"

I nod. Remember that she can't see me. "Yes. It's me. I'm at Saint-Laurent. I need you. I'm really fucked up and I don't want to go home. I don't have any bus money and I used the last of my change to call you."

She sighs, long and sad. I know she's disappointed in me, and it stings. "Don't be mad, Spence. Please. I'm sorry."

"I'm not mad," she says gently. "I'm worried about you. Stay there and I'll be there in like fifteen minutes in an Uber, okay?"

The lights flicker in the booth I'm in, a product of my emotions – I affect electricity, for some reason. "Okay. I'll be here."

When I get into the Uber, I feel Spencer's emotions hit me. They always do that, punch me in the gut, smack me in the face; leave me breathless.

She's feeling negativity so high that it's physically painful for me to be around her. But I need her. I need her so much.

"Spencer," I start sobbing right in front of the driver, "I'm don't feel well."

"I know you don't, baby," she says, reaching for me. "Come here. Put your head in my lap."

I do as I'm told. Keep crying. "The voices are so loud Spencer. I thought that going to the concert would help. I thought getting fucked up would help."

The voices are so loud tonight.

"It never helps," she replies calmly. "You should know that by now. And I see you hurt yourself again."

I nod. Shake my head. Nod again. "I don't know anything."

Spencer sighs again. "Whatever."

I know she's pissed off because I can feel it. She's pretending not to be, for my benefit, which hurts more somehow.

"Spence, I know when you're mad at me."

"I'm not mad," she says.

But I push. "Yes, you are."

"Let's not do this in front of the Uber driver, maybe?" she says, her voice hitching on the last word.

But I push her.

"You are mad, though."

"Cayden," she says in warning. "Don't."

"But you are."

"Fine! I'm mad!" she shouts, as we reach our destination, Spencer's and Ana's apartment complex.

We get out of the Uber, and she grabs me by the arm and drags me into the building. "I am furious," she says, when we get to her door. "I want to ring your neck. You need help, Cayden! Help that isn't me! You need therapy!"

I'm crying even more now because she's right. I do need help.

She sits me on the couch and gets out the appropriate bandages to wrap the wounds on my arms.

"Cayden, I love you, but when you hurt yourself it hurts me too. You have to know that!"

"I'm sorry," I sob. "I'm sorry."

She's not done yet. "What if one day you die because I'm not there to come get you in time? You could have a heart attack or wander off into traffic or something. I don't know."

She's so right. What if one day she isn't there in time? What if one day she doesn't answer the phone? What am I going to do then?

"I'm sorry."

"Stop apologising!" she shouts. "It means nothing without actions. Do you understand?"

I nod. I understand.

She bandages me and sends me home in an Uber I don't deserve.

I cry myself to sleep.

I wake up to my dad screaming at me. it ends with me on the ground, him over me, staring down at what he's done.

"Shit," he says, helping me up. "I didn't mean it."

"I know," I tell him, wounded and bleeding.

I'm late for school because of him.

When I get to school, I feel Spencer's Energy close by. Kessler is busy getting my file when she pops into the room, clearly looking for something.

She's surprised to see me.

Negativity also wafts off of her, and I wonder what she could be upset about.

"Hey...I shouldn't have shouted at you," she tells me, and my eyes widen, tears filling them, fast. "It's just you're so in tune with how I feel most of the time because you can see energy, that I guess I figured I didn't need to tell you how worried I was, because I thought you knew already."

My tears spill over, I bite my bottom lip to stop it from trembling. "Gods," I hiccup. "I'm so embarrassed right now."

"But I realize now that hearing it probably means something too, doesn't it?"

My eyes meet hers for a moment, before darting away again. "Yeah. It means a lot, Spence."

"I know I should stop doing stupid shit and hurting myself, but it's so hard sometimes, living in this skin. And i-it," my whole face is turning red, "it means a lot that you care enough about me to even get that upset. I guess I hadn't noticed because I didn't want to but that's no excuse. I know you worry about me, and I hate that I make you worry. But thanks for apologising. About the yelling..."

I'm quiet a bit before I say, "So, I'm uh, late. Again."

She nods her head, not pushing me for answers as to why. She and I both know one of my eyelids is darker than it was yesterday, and my bottom lip is slightly swollen where a cut is beginning to heal.

She bites her lip in sympathy. "I can see that. You kinda look like you feel like shit."

"I do feel like shit," I chuckle. "But don't worry about it. You know I've had worse."

She scoffs. "You're unbelievable, did you know that? Of course, I'm going to worry about you. Somebody has to."

I open my mouth to argue but stop when Spencer shoots me a look. A muscle in my jaw ticks, as I grind my teeth.

"You're going to shatter them pearly whites if you don't stop clenching your jaw," she taunts me. "Bet the dentist loves you."

I roll my eyes, but unclench, taking in a deep breath. "Dunno," I shoot back. "Never been."

"Where's Kessler?" Spencer changes subjects.

I run a hand through my hair. "Getting my file, I think. I'll probably be suspended thanks to my stunt yesterday, which is why I was just crying before your ass made me cry even more. Or, did you forget?"

"The guy had his hand on her ass though! That makes no sense!" Spencer yells, angry.

I'm silent for a while, but eventually I say, "Spence, you know how most people are sorta nervous around me?"

She nods, unsure as to where I'm going with this.

"Why can't I turn it off like you did?"

"I don't know. I don't understand how it happened. People just started reacting differently to me one day. I mean they're still totally freaked out by my existence or whatever, but they're not as....affected. Maybe it's because we're around people like us, now?"

I take a deep breath, and let it out. "I mean, me and you, we're not like anybody else, but we're not entirely like each other either, right?"

She nods. I'm right.

"And I try to do the right things, so people know I'm not going to, I dunno, go Dawson on their asses – I know I don't smile very often, but that's 'cause there's not a damn thing to smile about when the world's on fire."

I grunt angrily. "I stop a guy from touching a girl and I'm the one who gets in trouble because I'm already labelled a problem child because of my difference in DNA." I sigh. "I wish I knew what was wrong with me so I could just fix it. People are wary of you still, but not as wary as they are of me. It's half my attitude and half whatever it is that we are. And I hate that I have no control over that half. The half that isn't like anybody else, even you. I don't understand it, and I can't control it."

"I'm sorry. Most people at school avoid you, Cayden, because of the serious fuck-off vibes you send out," she tells me. "Not because of what we are, and not because you're a spark plug. You're just unwilling to get too close to anybody. Seriously, kids here aren't as bad as at our old school. You know, our friends have become friends with each other at this point. The only thing stopping the two groups from joining, is you."

"There's nothing wrong with you, Cayden," she tells me. "We're different, yeah. But what's wrong with being unique?"

"I don't want to be unique!" I shout, rather loudly, causing her to wince, just slightly. "You don't have to deal with the same things I do, Spence. I know you can sense people's auras and shit too, but there are things I don't tell you; you know, things that are unique to me? Things I can't understand because I can't find anybody who fits my description. I'm sure it's the same for you, that you can do more than what you've shown me, even if you don't know how to control it yet." I look away, indignant, but a bit embarrassed too.

"Okay, you're right that I haven't told you everything, but I don't know any more than you do. I mean I have theories, but they all sound freaking insane."

When my eyes meet hers again, I sigh. "Didn't mean to get mad. I just hate being so in the dark."

"S'okay." She smiles, wobblily.

I beckon her closer, holding out a tissue from Kessler's desk as a peace offering. "Your nose is running 'cause you're keeping back your tears. Not a good look," I say gently.

"Shut up," she sniffs.

"We will learn things, I guess," I relent. "It's just so damn hard sometimes to live life not understanding why we're here. How are you so confident? I mean, I don't even have any theories."

She's embarrassed. "I'm not that confident in myself," she's blushing, "but as a team we've always been good at connecting the dots."

I grin at her. "We always have been."

My eyes catch on her pen.

"I was nervous about doing the announcements." She scrambles for an excuse as to why she left it there. "When I came back to get it you were..."

"I gave you this pen," I muse, looking it over. "In fifth grade. How do you still have it? Does it even work?"

She looks like she wants to rip it out of my hands. "It gives me good luck on tests and stuff."

"I don't know that I believe in luck," I say, almost to myself, as I passes her the pen. "But you do you."

"Well, then I guess you don't want me to wish you luck with Kessler?"

Kessler is standing behind Spencer and I don't know what to say.

I grimace. "Actually, I take that back. I'm going to need all the luck I can get. You should probably get to class though."

"Yes," says Kessler's voice from behind Spencer. "Move along now, Miss Walker. Your male friend and I have some things we need to discuss that do not involve you, at least this time." More gently, he says, "I believe you can't supply Mr. Evander with an alibi today, as you weren't with him during the incident, I'm afraid. I understand he was standing up for someone, but physical violence is not tolerated here. I'm simply following procedure. Hendrick is suspended indefinitely, so Cayden is really getting off with a slap on the wrist. I'm not as bad as you kids think. I understand that Cayden's life at home is rough, as is your own."

Spencer and I both flinch at the reminder.

"But we don't see you fighting in the halls, do we Miss Walker?"

"No sir," she mumbles, voice coming out more sarcastic than intended.

"And why is that?"

She smiles, sweetly. "I don't have the balls, sir. But Cayden sure does."

Kessler laughs and waves her off. "Just get to class, okay?"

I make eye contact with Spencer, smile at her, and then I wave goodbye.

"Later, Pinky."

She smiles. "Later, Brain."

"You can stay until lunch," Kessler says to me once Spencer has walked away. "But then after that, you'll need to head home, son. I really am sorry that the protocol is so antiquated. Now, get to class you faux delinquent and get an education."

"Rodger that," I tell him, sending him a salute hat he finds just a bit funny – he doesn't hide his smile.

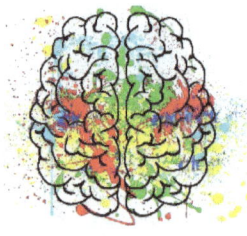

UNTITLED

SYDNIE BEAUPRÉ

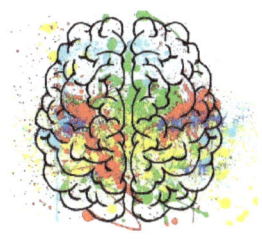

BIG ROCK

SYDNIE BEAUPRÉ

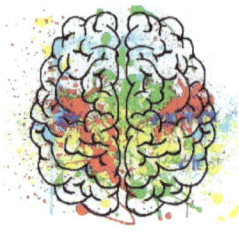

SUMMER

SYDNIE BEAUPRÉ

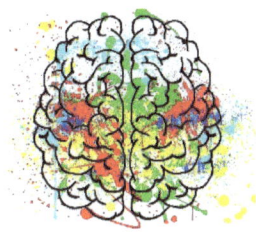

METRO DREAM

SYDNIE BEAUPRÉ

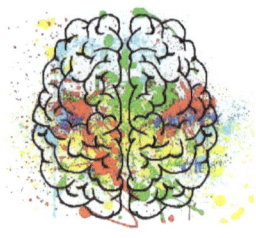

BLACK AND WHITE
SYDNIE BEAUPRÉ

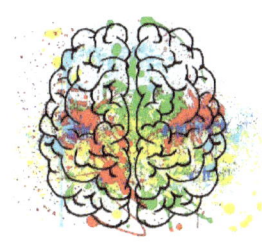

SKULL

SYDNIE BEAUPRÉ

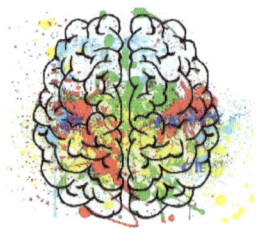

LINES

SYDNIE BEAUPRÉ

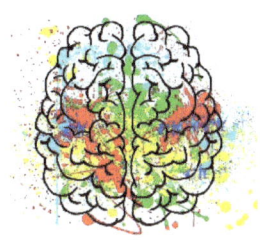

LOCK

SYDNIE BEAUPRÉ

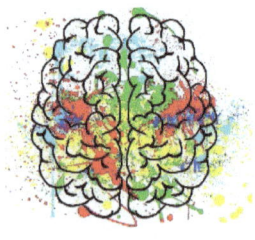

FOX

SYDNIE BEAUPRÉ

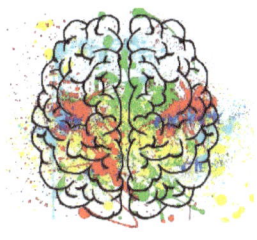

HEART

SYDNIE BEAUPRÉ

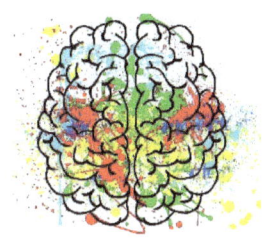

SHELL

MORGAN HILL

Is it me? Is it over? Are we there yet? Is he in college? Are we free? It's too fast, he's too old, only three-and-a-half more years. Either way he'll be gone, we'll be alone. Sweet Jesus, quiet.

No more being forced to listen to misogynistic rap, watching TikTok, blaring NBA2K and Madden. No late-night ride requests, no school Open Houses and parent conferences, no checking or enforcing homework. I won't have to email teachers or the attendance office. There will be no slammed doors, or *I hate you*, yelled with vitriol. No mortally wounded mama with each spit out insult from a know-it-all teen.

But then what? Moving to western Massachusetts, back to where I went to college, my dream. No empty nesting but nesting as a later-in-life romance, our first time together as husband and wife alone. New jobs, new lives, new identities, a 300-year-old house.

Parenting forever but from afar, hands on virtually. What will it be like to sleep naked with my love on a Wednesday night, no fear of being walked in on? Watch a show all the way through without umpteen knocks on the door with inane requests or teenager-y things like just telling us how annoying we are even though we are in the confines of our bedroom. Sweet relief. I can't fucking wait.

And yet...my baby. He still sometimes wants to cuddle under a blanket and watch a movie or hold hands as we walk, as long as we're far enough out of town that no one he knows nobody will see us, like we're having an adult affair. He relishes a "Mom and Me Day," just us. But as a 47-year-old newlywed, I also relish "Husband and Wife Day," also just us and so very difficult to come by. I'm caught.

Where does the medium fall here? The teen, self-proclaimed Most Impatient Person is beyond demanding of my time and jealous of that I spend with my husband. I don't do well under the thumb of a 9th grader and crave proximity of my partner.

Activities the teen and I enjoy together are harder to come by as he grows. No longer am I the picker of the activity but the negotiator. Usually we end up at the arcade or pier for a million dollars, eating out or me watching him video game in 15 minute increments because I don't want to learn how to play. He can be really sweet, endearing even, but as a teen he's also highly critical which makes him unpleasant to spend time with and leaves me feeling bad about myself because I eventually snap when he berates me: "Can you not scuff your shoes like that when you walk?" "You should dress like the other moms," "Mom, drink like a lady." STOP! ENOUGH! "Why do you even want to spend time with me? All you do is complain about me and then ask me for more money. That's not how this works. That's not how I raised you." Right? Right, I ask myself? Is this teenage or a horrific, decades-long parenting fail? I did The Classes, read The Books, Did The Things, put him in The Right Schools. Is this my fault? Part of it is his diagnosis of Oppositional Defiance Disorder, in which a child is unusually uncooperative, defiant, and hostile, exacerbated by his severe ADHD.

In contrast, my husband adores me. Where the teen drills holes the husband fills them. We complete each other, good and bad. It's not all hunky dory but most of it is. We do fight, but it's short-lived and usually because I have misinterpreted a passing glance or a tone, nothing big. My feelings get hurt but I know he loves me and everything will quickly be okay and our love is never in danger. We do almost everything together, flea markets, photography and meals out, to the point we discuss how we need to make more friends, branch out. But there's no one we'd rather spend time with than each other. There's been more than one time we've dressed alike, to our horror. I've picked up his facial expressions, and we've picked up each other's phrases, can finish each other's sentences. Walking to date night recently he looked up at the sky and said "That looks like a Magritte cloud. It looks like it should have an" "apple" we both said, under it. Yet we're not 90, barely 50. We're in a rented home, not a nursing home. I want more of that, less of mothering. Is that awful, my dream? Accountable only to each other and ourselves. Of course, this dream is on the worst days, moments.

Still, I dream of running away. What if I just left? What if I just left as the teen raged? Took some thrift store cashmere, jeans and flip flops, drove as far and fast as my midlife purchased red Mini would take me? Turned off my phone so his belligerent texts wouldn't reach me: "Such a little bitch. Of course you run away like you always do. I fucking hate you." I'd pay in cash so I couldn't be traced. But I wouldn't do that to my husband. Probably. But I've been on the brink with a bag packed and a destination scouted way more than once. But then I get a fleeting moment with the kid. An "I love you" or a hug. It's just enough to make me rethink giving up entirely.

At home, I steel myself weekly or more with adult beverages and try to enforce him cleaning his pigsty and doing his laundry, both of which he should be doing himself, but I end up doing because it's easier than fighting with him. He resists and yells and slams his door. When he doesn't have clothes to wear he tantrums. I should teach him to cook and stop listening to him bitch he doesn't like what we prepare and let him figure it out. But I don't. Because he's generally an asshole, and I can't just quit him because my mom instinct is ultimately stronger than my desire to run away.

The days are long, but the years are short. I hated that expression when my kid was young because both parts of it are true. The days are longer now because he stays up until midnight instead of six and we get no relief. The years are shorter only because the college countdown is on but they still seem to last forever, whereas seven years of courtship with my new husband flew by. Two sets of time seem to exist. Five months of newlywed life? Gone in a snap. The first five months of high school? Forever.

Every morning of waking him up and getting him out the door takes years. Battle-scarred from it, I collapse on my sofa with another cup of coffee at 7:40 a.m. Monday through Friday, having just been through the Five Stages of Teen School Wake Up: Denial, Anger, Screaming, Fighting, and Door Slamming.

Weekend mornings with my husband involve lingering in bed with a second cup and some *New York Times* puzzles and Wordle, scrolling Facebook, small talk and planning which flea markets and Goodwills to hit up. I wish these mornings could last forever. Child-free weekends when he is with his dad are what we live for. Breweries and every meal out are a budget-busting luxury but a sanity-saving one. Soon it will end too quickly. We will go back to parenting. But until then we feel like adults: carefree, living an imaginary life of no responsibilities, day drinking and eating cheese and bread in bed and having loud sex without worry of traumatizing the kid who doesn't even want us to kiss.

Whereas my teen craves "surprises" every time I go out, junk that entertains him for minutes, my husband enjoys permanence. He shopped for his wedding ring a couple months before we got married, put it on in the store and has never taken it off. My kid constantly has demands, my husband has none. My son drives me to the brink, raising my pulse, my husband is my safe haven, raising it for a different reason. I want to run away from my teen. I want to run away with my husband.

Quickly, the kid is back Sunday and we're back to reality for two weeks until he goes to dad again. There is no relief in sight. No break except Wednesday night sushi and Sunday night Mexican date nights. Sometimes we'll go out on weekends alone but even then, the teen constantly calls with anxiety of when we'll be home. And then he abuses us. Oppositional Defiance Disorder is no joke.

My husband is the better parent naturally but maybe because he's been at it less time. I don't think he wants to run away but has also asked me to get a door handle with a lock for his office the next time I'm at the hardware store. I feel like my heart sometimes is locked down to protect myself from further hurt. I have breakthrough anxiety chest pains, despite medication, from having to deal with my son. Go to college. Never leave.

Is it me? Is it him? I think it's us. In a weird relationship in which we both need help. I want to flee half the time. He hates me the other half. The other half I just want to be with my beloved, not with my son. He just went from the sweetest boy in the world, golden curls and soft baby rolls, to not and I feel it's me. Maybe it's teen? "It makes me feel good when you get upset. I do things to upset you like say no to trips and activities so you keep asking me to go. It makes me feel good." I try to remember the mental illness component but I the moment I'm a failure. I give in too often to just make it stop and then feel shame. It's a vicious circle, a snake eating its tail.

I'm naturally attracted to the word "grit" because I don't have any. I need to learn some and apply it because it's all going by slow and fast. When he's hurling obscenities at me I'm so paralyzed I can barely move, like I'm sinking in quicksand. But yesterday I was in the hospital holding him for the first time, thinking about how glad I was to have a boy because they always love their mothers. I'm in the last years and I don't want to regret them. He often says he doesn't feel I love him anymore. I do. Mostly. But I need to dig my heels in until I do truly and that will take work on my part because I don't know I can expect him to change without the treatment he refuses. Because all too soon it will be over and too late. And I need to send him out knowing I loved him most of all.

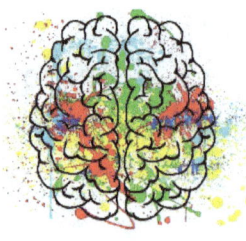

WORLD I SURRENDER YOU

NICKSON ODONGO MAGAK

Of the world break my heart

Payless work tire my brains

World entomb hopes.

The loved bring me to tears

Friends hypocratic envious

Penury you handicap me;

Un-man me to a thing of rags,

Rob me of life

I rightfully own.

You live forever,

I live today a derelict

Epical omniscient dead leaves

Sunlight has nothing to brighten

Night nothing to hide.

You are but aromatic chamber

In which my sterile expression

Indexed to store in stagnant admiration

Veil of my face

Decrepitated at childish dream.

My unworthy existence, an indication

That you care

Perhaps tomorrow would wake up to sanity

A little repose

Then I would be whom I wanted

For today I surrender you.

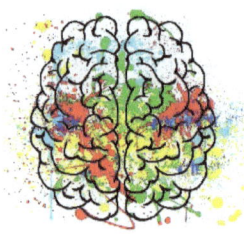

ENDURING MOMENTS

NICKSON ODONGO MAGAK

Friendly hands hesitant greet

Silence communication scents tough times

The moment rearing descent secret

Transforming landscape blues

Emptying final stock in scarcity

Hope, enduring hostility

Feasting of remains of dead end

When nothing goes to waste.

Of beautiful harvest and tower of wealth,

Would want to fantasise

Yet harshest times on earth punishes

Hope looked by life in years.

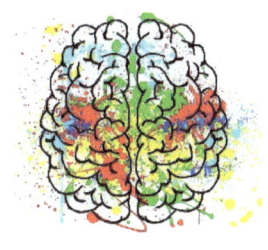

TRIALS
NICKSON ODONGO MAGAK

Sprouting gouts of weak mind

Shaking ciders stinking the wind

Smooth light winds that blow the legs

At the corner, pots are moulding in mosh.

Animals graze without herders

Feasting calves take long to discover grass

Hands too weak to milk their mothers

Pitiless piety, our villages eaten

"To be a Christian you must be crazy"

Like flesh into crocodiles jaws,

Spanking paws seeking refuge

Ending up in a mash without cash

"Where's our God we crash."

History cannot spy it all

A spitted dog does not nose hunt

The haunting biters' barrow

Birds singing, human sin in kinship

Humans cry, dear God!

Why did you create we if it's like this?

I take "Nyanam" to fill the pots

"Thuon" is soon returning home

Orphans naked statue stare

Halfly covered by blankets abandoned

By sane madmen.

They'll soon have strong hands;

Calves will graze

Burrows will be buried-dogs freed

"Your sorrows are not forever

Am the lasting ever

Trials and temptations prior apple

I never abandon my people."

---

* Nyanam: A Luo word meaning, the daughter of the Lake.

**Thuon: A Luo pun meaning a Cock or a brave person

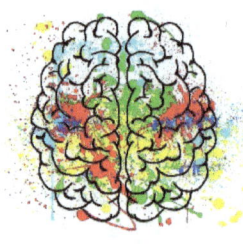

DISTANT CONSTELLATION
NICKSON ODONGO MAGAK

Staring space obliquely

Fumbling eating with eye

Munching the taste

Distant within reach

Sterile existence mocks manhood.

The very life's survival turmoil

Eroded already fragile psyche

Childhood dreams disintegrate

Like schoolboy prank's cynical imagination.

Distant constellations

Recreating childhood

Lost to haunting ghost

Realities slippery to grasp.

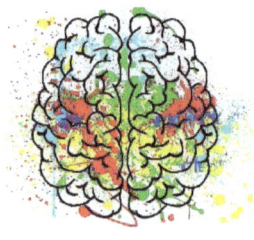

LISTEN TO THE CANDLE

CHRIS FRIEND

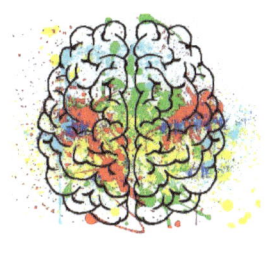

DEVOUR THE SUN

CHRIS FRIEND

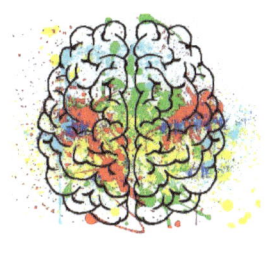

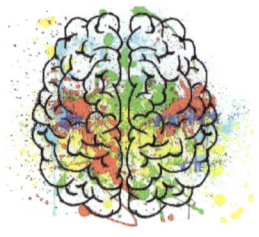

CATS

CHRIS FRIEND

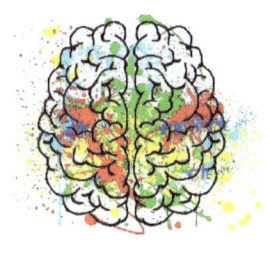

DESADE GRAVE HEAD

CHRIS FRIEND

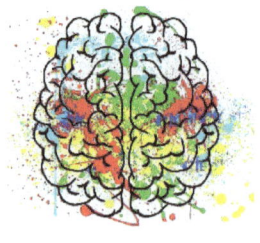

EGG

CHRIS FRIEND

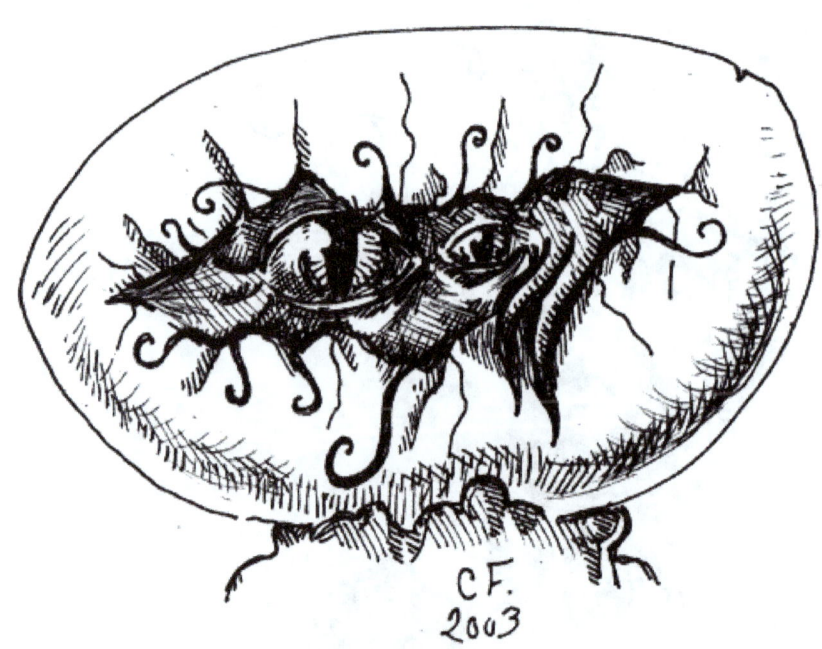

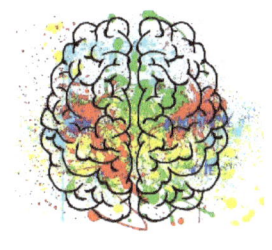

MUMMY

CHRIS FRIEND

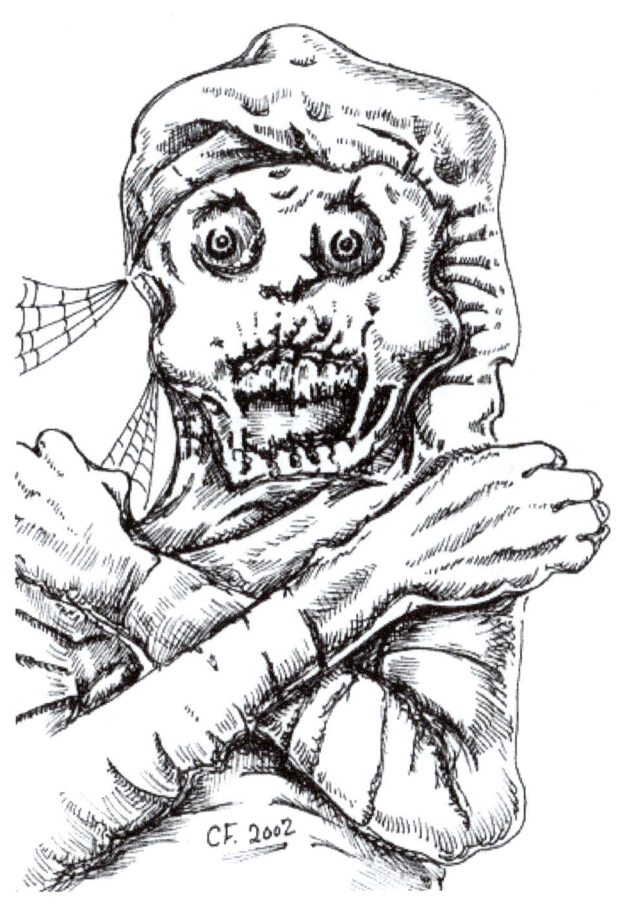

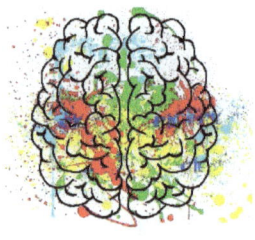

MONSTER CHILD

CHRIS FRIEND

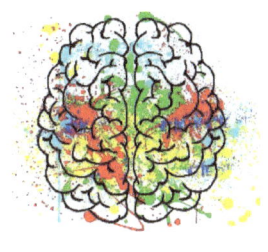

MOONMAN

CHRIS FRIEND

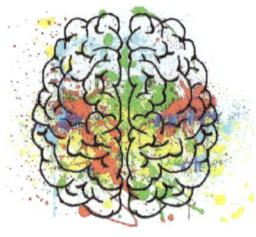

ONE HORN

CHRIS FRIEND

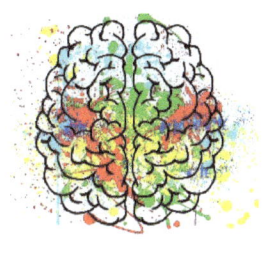

DEAD

CHRIS FRIEND

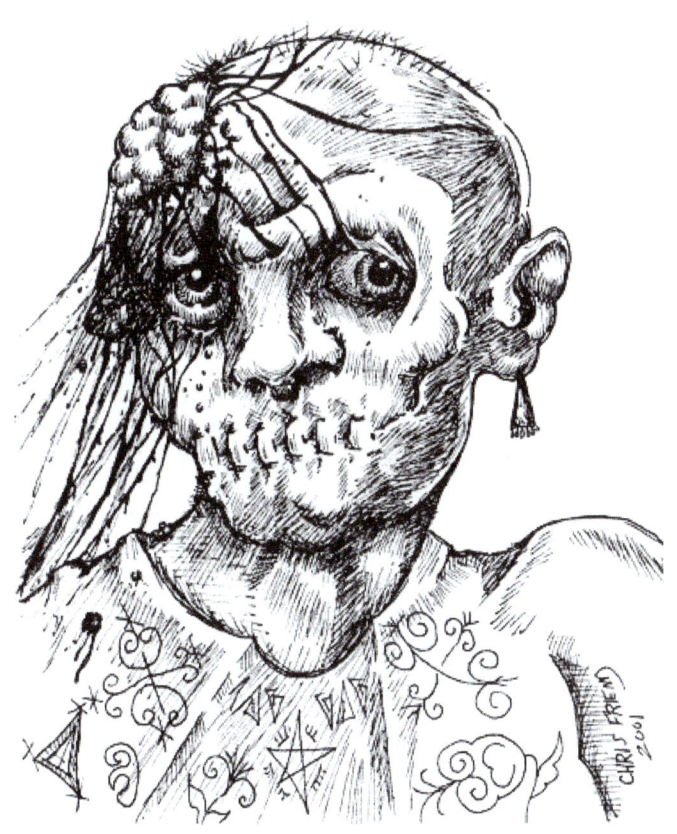

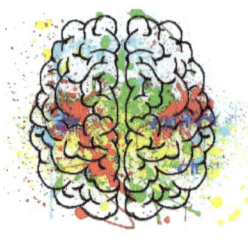

TALK & SELF TALK
DAN FLORE III

"I don't know what is happening."

you're just smoking a cigarette Dan

smoke your cigarette

relax

remember your mother and father waving to you from the
boardwalk when you were a calm and happy as a little boy

wave back

you're still like that

that's still you

this isn't happening

you're ok

do your breathing

like your learned in the hospital

you're ok

you're ok

"Jesus."

exactly you're going to be needing a lot of Him

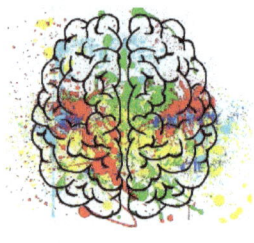

LURASIDONE

VINCENT ST. CLARE

Trudging the miles between pain and principle

On sacred Safa I fell down

A jagged outcrop took out my brain

But on the golden slopes of Marwa I was restored

When I laid down again

Oscillations against the indifference of the stars

Vibrations running from helplessness to intimations of hope

On the crest of that hill I laid there headless yet living

Numb yet seeking

For what?

A long way gone
My heart beats out of my chest
Then slows as I watch thin clouds supply
Shadows to the desert

A higher light begs for my presence
Or was it I who called to her?
Deep to deep
A tragedy played out in triumphing over
the adversity of splintering seconds

But where should I find the will to look up
When I have to watch my steps so carefully?

I worry I might fall on my way between
Agony and insensibility

I who see without eyes know

This path to have grown shorter

The wrath of time and light dulled

For quarters at the pharmacy

But what grander truth have I lost in my cold?

What fails to know me, and I it?

What stars no longer favor my sight?

What sky does not receive me?

I preach dust for the sake of freedom

I speak a vanished creativity for the price

Of the suggestion of peace

Four corners once again stabilize the

Deep of the teetering world

Yet Earth is not a verdant green from down here

In the cold I cast bones to the aether

Divining minutes that might occur centuries from now

But what can I say?

That's the best a pill supplies to the drowned

I choked on sand and dust in the desert of my mind

These little mountains may do little wonders

Yet in the end they just don't suffice

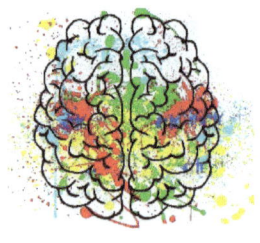

SOON

VINCENT ST. CLARE

I stand on no hill

I revoke your peak

I crawl a little ways up

To sample the slope of the valley

I slide back down again

Left with my morsel

I'll stay and die

Starve and wind about myself

Nothing is the best present you can find here

What words can be spoken to ameliorate the dread here?

God shot us down to dust

God shat us up to truth

The birds are besides themselves

The children are playing with dirt

Leave us with our stones and glory

Leave us with our rocks and and stones

Leave us with our leaves and things

Leave us with our graves and tombs

Death is a future

Death is a mantra

Linea viridis gyrat universa?

I tasted the shame of being something

Only to become no-one

I reveled in the realization of true love

Only to find myself taken away with a storm

I was with God for a moment just to

Never see nor hear from her again

And now I ask

What hill I should stand on

Every day flat and unyielding the same

Beaten out washed up gray land

I thought I scrambled up a slope here or there

To take a taste

But it was flat dust in my teeth

A mirage to the mind

A gun to the head

And the birds besides themselves, still

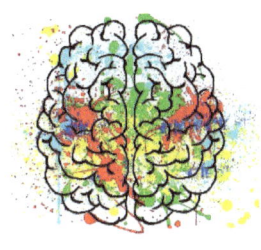

LOVE *PER SE*
VINCENT ST. CLARE

Between pain and
Principle

The real
Struggle

Your feet hit the floor
And then a resounding
"Yes"

Forms and echoes and
Throughout time

Dissipates and dies

At the close of the day

Eyes closed

Heart on fire

Head on wheels

Life must be lived!

Life broken and bottomed out

Life strange and stranger still

Life bottlenecked and burned up

Run while you choke

And laugh while you die

You'll feel better looking back

I'm sure

And may you earn a perfect moment,

—Or at least a soft deathbed—

And may you learn to love

As you've ever loved

Nothing at all,
Nothing *always*

In that dream would you
Sink through your grave
And on the other side

Begin once again?

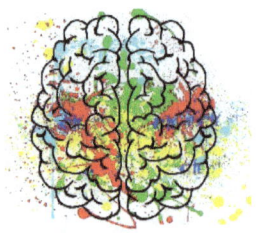

BUT FAMILY

ADIYAAN KHANDAKAR

Family is complicated

You see

We fight sometimes

But we love hard

Our voices can get loud

But our hearts are big

Family is complicated

But I wouldn't trade mine

Not for money or fame or power

You see

Family is forever

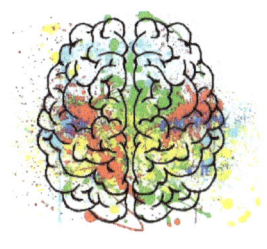

GRADUATION DAY
ADIYAAN KHANDAKAR

Onto the next

Adventure

He goes triumphantly

Celebrated by those he loves

Eager for what's to come

Crowds sing a soft melody

Tears gather in our mothers' eyes

A new chapter emerges

And I continue

To rise

Up up up

And away I go

Victorious

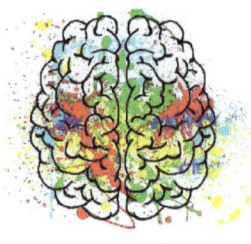

ART

ADIYAAN KHANDAKAR

Art a universal language

Speaks to me

In colourful whispers

Abstract

Just like me

Beloved

All the same

Each painting

Each human

Unique

As it should be

Art is within us all

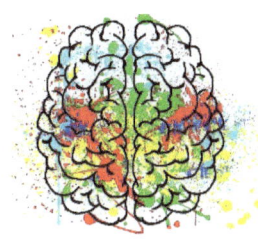

FREEDOM THE ULTIMATE GOAL

ADIYAAN KHANDAKAR

Freedom

Over one's life

What a prize I'm told

Freedom

We can't stop

Until all behold.

Freedom

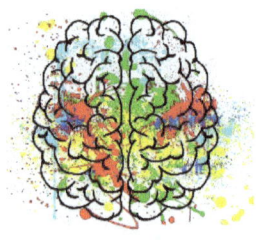

FOR MY PERSON
ADIYAAN KHANDAKAR

My mom

So fierce

And strong

She marvels

Everyone

Her smile

Makes my world

Go around

Her embrace my safest place

My mom

My guide

My person

I love you

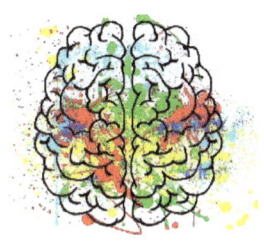

A MOTHER'S EMBRACE
ADIYAAN KHANDAKAR

A mother's embrace

The safest haven

Through any storm

Her arms, a shield

Protecting me

Her words, a pacifier

Soothing me

In my mother's embrace

It's safe to be me

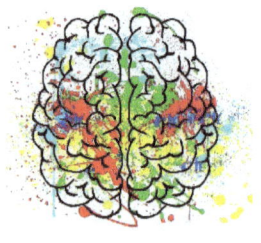

A MYTH

ADIYAAN KHANDAKAR

in mount olympus there was many gods. each with their own special powers. these gods ruled down in earth. zeus was the king of the olympians, hera his queen. the mortals had caused some trouble down on earth. they had been polluting the ocean, which made posiden very angry. posiden was not a kind man when angry. he would start massive tsunamis just to punish the people. often killing some in its wake. the people begged for forgiveness from the gods.

zeus was reluctant, he wondered if they had actually learned their lesson. to test the mortals he asked them to complete some tasks. task one was to rid of plastic straws. they were getting stuck in the turtles noses and killed them. task two was to stop using plastic bags. they were suffocating the fish so the population had decreased significantly.

zeus had little hope that they would succeed. he gave them one month to complete these tasks, if they didn't comply he would send them all down to hades the god of the underworld. this may seem harsh, but the truth was if they didnt clean up their planet, they would all die anyways. one month flew by quickly, but the humans had not quite made their goals. that being said they had made some serious efforts.

zeus rather than sending the mortals down to hades sentenced them to stay with their dying planet. he wanted them to live with the damage they had created. ecosystems disappeared one by one until the earth was bare. the mortals quickly went extinct, and the gods had to start again.

this is not just a myth. we are in a mass extinction. we need to act now, our earth is begging us. how dare you ignore us? the children you claim to love. help us.

the end

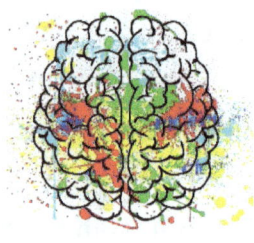

UNDER DEPRESSION, I CAN'T LIVE EASILY
MAID CORBIC

every day is a horror
for me the story is sad
when I have no friends around me
who will be there with me always
whenever necessary

I can only say one thing to myself
and that is that I am brave when I have the guts
to say aloud that some worries bother me
of a teenage nature, time does not go to my hand

everyone around me became happy
strained lives and married for a reason
only I still tread in my place
watching and applauding everyone around him

have I fallen now on all that from life
I went through all sorts of things somehow
but I get depressed because no one is there
to comfort me when it's hardest

it is possible that I am a strange man and a young link
who must understand that the world is like that
ready to still make me gloomy
for I am someone who believes again that behind darkness
there is a light bulb

I was the strongest when I had someone with me
but it is impossible that no one loves me as I am
do you judge me for my success now?
is it fortunate that others are getting along easily now?

it's a shame that the rainbows make fun of me too
but the modern era is this and a world without borders
where every day I look from where it is clear
and I laugh to myself during the day
and in the evening I cry because it is hard for me
to continue to be a happy young man!

Thank you for reading Fusion: Better Together. If you liked what you read, please leave a review, and recommend the book to a friend or family member. It would mean the world for the contributors and me.

Thank you,

Sydnie

www.ingramcontent.com/pod-product-compliance
Lightning Source LLC
Chambersburg PA
CBHW070503030726
47503CB00004B/1153